THE BAMBOO SWORD
AND OTHER SAMURAI TALES

THE BAMBOO SWORD

AND OTHER SAMURAI TALES

Shuhei Fujisawa

Translated by
Gavin Frew

KODANSHA INTERNATIONAL
Tokyo • New York • London

This book has been selected by the Japanese Literature Publishing Project (JLPP), which is run by the Japanese Literature Publishing and Promotion Center (J-Lit Center) on behalf of the Agency for Cultural Affairs of Japan.

The stories in this collection were originally published in Japanese, and were selected from the following publications: "The Bamboo Sword" (*Takemitsu shimatsu*, 1981) from *Takemitsu shimatsu* (Shinchosha, Tokyo 1981); "A Passing Shower" (*Hashiri ame*, 1980) from *Hashiri ame* (Shinchosha, Tokyo 1985); "All for a Melon" (*Ikka no uri*, 1976) from *Enzai* (Shinchosha, Tokyo 1982); "Kozuru" (*Kozuru*, 1979) from *Kamikakushi* (Shinchosha, Tokyo 1983); "Shinza, the Samurai" (*Hesomagari Shinza*, 1976) from *Enzai* (Shinchosha, Tokyo 1982); "Out of Luck" (*Un no tsuki*, 1980) from *Hashiri ame* (Shinchosha, Tokyo 1985); "The Runaway Stallion" (*San no maru hiroba gejo doki*, 1987) from *Mugiyamachi hirusagari* (Bungeishunju, Tokyo 1992); "Dancing Hands" (*Odoru te*, 1988) from *Yoru kieru* (Bungeishunju, Tokyo 1994)

Distributed in the United States by Kodansha America, Inc., and in the United Kingdom and continental Europe by Kodansha Europe Ltd.

Published by Kodansha International Ltd., 17–14 Otowa 1-chome, Bunkyo-ku, Tokyo 112–8652, and Kodansha America, Inc.

Copyright © 1981 1980, 1976, 1979, 1976, 1980, 1987, 1988 by Kazuko Kosuge. English translation copyright © 2005 by Gavin Frew.
All rights reserved. Printed in Japan.
ISBN-13: 978-4-7700-3005-4
ISBN-10: 4-7700-3005-3

First edition, 2005
12 11 10 09 08 07 06 05   10 9 8 7 6 5 4 3 2 1

Library of Congress Catalogue-in-Publication Data available

www.kodansha-intl.com

CONTENTS

The Bamboo Sword	7
A Passing Shower	41
All for a Melon	57
Kozuru	99
Shinza, the Samurai	129
Out of Luck	169
The Runaway Stallion	185
Dancing Hands	237

The Bamboo Sword

The young guard had been keeping an eye on the family ever since it first appeared in the square beyond the castle's outer gate. The family consisted of a samurai, his wife, and two young children holding their mother's hands. They were dressed in threadbare clothes.

As they drew nearer the gate, the guard saw that his first impression of poverty had been correct. However, he was struck as much by the beauty of the wife as by the sorry state of their clothing. Few women in the town could rival her in looks. He stood watching them fixedly until he realized they were heading straight for the gate.

"And where might you be going?" he demanded officiously. His tone was severe, but he used the polite form of address because although the family looked extremely poor, the man wore two swords revealing his samurai status.

A river ran past the main gate of Unasaka Castle, creating an impressive moat sixty feet across. When the castle was built, the river had been deepened and both banks strengthened with stone walls. A wooden bridge across the moat provided access from the town to the castle. On the town side of the moat was a small wooden gateway manned by a few guards, while the main gate on the other side was an imposing two-story building, with huge doors and a heavy, tiled roof.

Besides this main gate, there were eleven other entrances into the castle's outer bailey, within which lay an inner bailey. Inside that was a central donjon that dominated the skyline. The castle had armories, powder magazines, storehouses for food in case of a siege, stables, and the domain's administrative offices. In the outer bailey there were also a number of houses belonging to senior retainers, providing an extra line of defense for the donjon.

The fact that people lived within the castle meant that they—as well as merchants, farmers, and others with business at the domain's offices—had to be allowed entry, and it was the duty of the guards at the outer gate to check the comings and goings of these people. The gate was open from five o'clock in the morning until five o'clock in the evening, but even during this period farmers had to receive permission each time they entered, while others had to present passes issued by the residence or the domain office they wished to visit. In order for the guards to confirm that the passes were genuine, all twelve gates of the castle had ledgers with samples of the various seals of authorization.

In this case, the suspicious attitude of the young guard was not merely a result of customary caution but also due to the family's evident poverty.

The man looked to be about thirty-five years old. He was wearing a samurai's black kimono bearing his family crest and had two swords thrust through the sash at his waist. His feet in their straw sandals were covered with dust, while the straw hat he held in one hand was old and had several holes. His wife and children also looked as if they had been on the road with him and had just arrived at the castle after a long journey. This was not unusual in itself, but closer inspection of their clothes revealed a mass of darns. The man's kimono had been washed so often that the family crest was faded almost to the point of being indiscernible.

Furthermore, all four family members looked exhausted. The man was in the worst condition of them all, and his sunken cheeks were covered with unkempt beard, making him appear all the more disreputable. It was difficult to imagine what business he might have in the castle.

"My name is Oguro Tanjuro," the man said, approaching the guard at the gate. His voice sounded unexpectedly cheerful. "I was once a retainer of Lord Matsudaira in Echizen. I wonder if you could help me."

"What is it you want?"

"I'm looking for a man by the name of Tsugé Hachirozaemon. I believe he holds a position here."

"Tsugé?" The young guard gazed at the sky in thought for a moment, but then remembered. "Yes, he resides here."

"He says he resides here," repeated Tanjuro, turning around to his family. They had been looking on with anxious expressions, but relief flooded into their faces when they heard this. They seemed overjoyed, and the children even skipped a few steps, all the time holding their mother's hands.

"Tsugé Hachirozaemon is the chamberlain of the domain."

"Did you hear that? He's the chamberlain," Tanjuro repeated, and his young family again capered with glee.

"Could you be so kind as to tell me where his house is located?" said Tanjuro, turning to the guard.

"He lives over there, in the outer bailey." The guard still regarded Tanjuro and his family dubiously. "But what is the nature of your business with him? Are you an acquaintance?"

"No, I've never had the honor of meeting him. However . . ." Tanjuro hurriedly reached inside his kimono and extracted four or five letters tied together with string. He licked his thumb and finger and sorted through them, selecting one with "Tsugé Hachirozaemon" written on it in bold black characters. He removed the letter and held it out for the guard to read.

"As you see, it's a letter of recommendation."

The guard scanned the contents quickly.

"So you are looking for a position?"

"Yes, that is so."

The guard scrutinized Tanjuro and his family once more. Now that he thought about it, he remembered that the domain had hired several samurai a month or so earlier, and there had been many men in much the same condition as Tanjuro coming and going. He had no idea where they had heard about the vacancies, but they all carried similar letters of recommendation and had been desperate to find work. However, that had been during the heat of July, so those positions had long been filled. Seeing the quiet expectancy on the faces of the pitiful little group before him, though, the guard did not want to be the one to disappoint them.

"I've been without a post for a long time now. We were staying with an acquaintance in the Aizu region when we heard about the vacancies here. Luckily, our acquaintance is a good friend of Tsugé Hachirozaemon, so we rushed here as fast as we could. It's a great relief to know that Tsugé is the chamberlain. Even our friend did not know that."

"You may pass," the guard said. Seeing that Tanjuro was about to put the recommendation letter back inside his kimono, he added, "You'd better keep that letter out to show the guards at the main gate."

He guessed that the guards there would also find Tanjuro's shabby state sufficient grounds to stop him. He watched as the family, now walking with a lighter step, made its way over the bridge.

"What was all that about, Hashimoto?" the guard's superior asked, unable to conceal the mirth in his voice as he came out of the guardroom. "Fool! Doesn't he know there's no more hiring? I hear they already took on five extra men."

"That's what I thought, but I didn't have the heart to tell them."

"No matter. They'll find out soon enough when they get to Tsugé's mansion."

It just so happened that the chamberlain, Tsugé Hachirozaemon, was away on official business that day, so Tanjuro did not manage to see him after all. On their arrival at Tsugé's residence the family was met by a young man who stared in disbelief at their tattered clothing and paid scant attention to Tanjuro's formal greetings before disappearing back into the house. His place was taken by a polite, rather plump woman in her mid-forties, who turned out to be the chamberlain's wife.

A look of puzzlement passed across her face when she first saw them, but her smile was warm. She listened to Tanjuro's speech of introduction and read the letter of recommendation he presented.

"I see," she said, "but I am afraid I have to disappoint you."

"Oh?"

"Unfortunately, my husband is away at the moment and will not be back for four or five days."

"Four or five days?" Tanjuro repeated with a sigh. His face crumpled, and for a moment she thought he was going to break down and weep, but he soon brought himself under control.

She realized that the family must have pinned all their hopes on her husband, and the sight of their threadbare clothes moved her to pity. She had never heard of Katayanagi Zusho, the man in Aizu who had recommended Tanjuro to her husband, and she had no idea whether there was a post available, but her heart went out to the family before her, proud in their bearing despite their evident poverty. The letter said that Tanjuro had been employed by the daimyo of Inuyama, Lord Hiraiwa, until he died without leaving an heir, which resulted in the disbandment of the clan. Tanjuro had then found a position with the Matsudaira clan of Echizen province. However, it was not the man's background but the sight of his wife and young children that touched the chamberlain's wife. Tanjuro's wife was slight in build and seemed no more than twenty years of age. She looked almost like a child herself, while her daughters, one aged five or six and the other about three, stood staring up at her with intelligent eyes. They were dressed in rags, but they still retained their pride as befitted their samurai status.

"My husband has gone to Konuma but will definitely return in four or five days. Can you wait until then?"

The town of Konuma, located by the sea some twenty miles from Unasaka, was the site of Kaionji Castle, one of the clan's subsidiary castles under the charge of a steward.

"Yes, we can wait. I will come again after he has returned."

"Do you know where you will stay?"

"No, we have no plans yet. We will look for a suitable inn."

"Why don't you stay here? If you have no objections, I'd be happy to see to your needs."

"No, we could not impose on you like that," Tanjuro said, shaking his head. "We came to ask a favor, and we couldn't possibly take advantage of your hospitality that way."

"In that case you must promise to come again after my husband has returned. I will put in a word on your behalf."

"We are most obliged." Tanjuro made a deep bow, and his wife and children did the same. As he was about to leave, he stopped and asked awkwardly, "May I trouble you to return my letter of recommendation?"

"Here you are," the chamberlain's wife replied, handing him the letter that had been lying open on her knees. She looked at him curiously. "But surely you will be giving it to my husband anyway?"

"That is true," Tanjuro said, putting his hand to his head in a gesture of embarrassment. "But it is very important to me."

She understood then just how vital the letter must be for the four of them, and she warmed to them even more. "Just a moment," she said as they turned to leave. "If you can't find a suitable inn, try the Tokiwaya in Yayoi. My husband goes there a lot so I'm sure you will be treated well there."

"You are most kind."

"Oh, I almost forgot something important."

Beckoning them back inside the entrance hall, she went to the rear of the house, reappearing a little later with a cloth-wrapped bundle and a letter.

"Please don't think me presumptuous, but I have packed some old clothes for you and also written a letter for you to show the guards at the gate the next time you come." She had guessed that Tanjuro might have trouble entering the castle given his present appearance, so she had written a few lines and affixed the household seal at the bottom of the letter to facilitate his passage.

Tanjuro thanked her once more and the family left, walking out through the main castle gate and over the bridge in silence. When they came to the square beyond the small outer gate, Tanjuro looked back and saw the guard there, stave in hand, watching them suspiciously.

"What shall we do now?" he asked, turning to his wife. His children were looking at him uneasily. "I thought that once we presented our case to Tsugé all our problems would be solved. I did not allow for the fact that he might not be home."

"At least we know he exists and that he is the chamberlain. So our worries are over," his wife said encouragingly, holding the package Tsugé's wife had given her. "We just have to wait four or five days."

"But how are we going to manage?" Tanjuro asked anxiously. Realizing their predicament, his wife lowered her eyes. They had entered the Unasaka domain the previous night and had spent the last of their money at an inn in Eguchi village. Earlier that day she had also exchanged her last item of value, a hair ornament, for some rice balls for lunch.

"Are there any rice balls left?" Tanjuro asked. As long as they had some food they could sleep under the eaves of a shrine that night.

This was the second time Tanjuro had been a ronin, as samurai who had no lord to serve were called. The first time was when Hiraiwa Shinkichi, the daimyo his family had served since his father's time, died on New Year's Eve in 1611 without a successor and the clan was disbanded. Ironically, the daimyo did have a son, but as his wife's father had fought on the wrong side in the Battle of Sekigahara in 1600, in which the great general Tokugawa Ieyasu won control of the entire country, Hiraiwa was wary of arousing the hostility of the new government and had refrained from registering him as his heir. As a reward for this gesture of loyalty, the shogun had given Hiraiwa his own seventh son, Matsuchiyo, as an heir, but the boy had died at the age of six and no other heir had been chosen.

Tanjuro was twenty years old when Hiraiwa died and he became a ronin. His father had already passed away, and he had his elderly mother and a young girl of ten to support. This girl, Tami, who was now his wife, had been orphaned at the age of four. Her father had also been a retainer of the Hiraiwa family, and when he and his wife died in rapid succession, Tanjuro's family took the girl in as they were her closest relatives.

After spending three years looking for another post, Tanjuro was fortunate enough to be offered employment by Yoshida Yoshihiro, a powerful retainer of the Matsudaira family of Echizen province, after being recommended by a former retainer of Hiraiwa. Luck was on his side as the Yoshidas were enlisting men for the winter siege of Osaka Castle, home to the Toyotomi clan, Shogun Tokugawa Ieyasu's nemesis and the most serious challenge to his authority.

The founder of the Matsudaira clan had moved from the territories he held in Shimosa to Echizen province in 1601, and received income from both places—500,000 bushels of rice from Shimosa and 2,800,000 bushels from Echizen. When he took over the latter, he divided the land among his leading retainers, and Tanjuro's employer, Yoshida Yoshihiro, was given land yielding 70,000 bushels annually, which made him not only a chief retainer but a minor lord in his own right.

However, in the summer of 1615, during the second and last siege of Osaka Castle, Yoshida committed suicide just before the final attack. He had been urging the lord the domain, Matsudaira Tadanao, to break rank and attack the following morning, before the rest of the army, and so win greater glory for the domain. Yoshida took full responsibility for this unlawful military maneuver and his ritual suicide was to atone for the deed. In view of these factors, Tanjuro was subsequently offered a new post by another principal retainer, the young Nagami Uemonnosuke.

Uemonnosuke was only nine years old when Tanjuro began to serve him, but with a fief worth 77,000 bushels of rice the boy was equal in rank to the chief councilor of the domain. Both his grandparents were related to the shogun, Tokugawa Ieyasu, and when the boy's father chose to follow his lord into death at the age of twenty-four, his retainers had banded together to protect the Nagami family.

Two years after taking his post with the Nagamis, Tanjuro married Tami, who was then sixteen years old. Three years later, his mother died after a long sickness. The following year their daughter was born, and Tanjuro felt that he would be happy to live in Echizen for the rest of his life. His income was only 150 bushels of rice a year, no comparison with the 900 bushels he had received with the Hiraiwa family, but he and Tami were content, and he never wanted to be a ronin again.

This was not to say that they had not heard rumors about the behavior of their lord, Matsudaira Tadanao, but never in their wildest dreams did they imagine that it would affect them.

When the end came, then, it was swift and in a form no one could have anticipated.

Matsudaira Tadanao had been highly praised by the first shogun, Tokugawa Ieyasu, for his courage during the two sieges of Osaka Castle. However, two years after the second siege, his wife Ocha—the third daughter of the second shogun, Hidetada—left the castle at Fukui and returned to her father in Edo, taking their son with her. From this time on, Tadanao's behavior began to draw comment. Tadanao and Ocha were both grandchildren of the first shogun, and Ocha had been given in marriage to Tadanao at the age of eleven. Their son was born when she was fifteen years old, but by the time she fled to Edo the marital relationship had fallen to such depths that Tadanao was rumored to have tried to kill her and the boy. After she left, he relied ever more heavily on the advice of his courtier Oyamada Tamon, the biggest sycophant in the domain. For his mistress, he took a woman he called Ikkoku Gozen, meaning "princess of the domain." The two were never apart, and the depravities they indulged in earned them a reputation for bloodthirstiness.

This "princess" derived pleasure from seeing people killed, so Tadanao ordered condemned criminals to be brought to the garden overlooked by his rooms in order that she could watch them be beheaded. When there was a shortage of condemned men, Tadanao had minor criminals killed for her enjoyment, eventually going so far as to set impossible tasks for his pages so he could put the sword to them himself when they refused to obey. He had a huge ball of burning moxa placed on the stomach of one page and sat watching as the boy screamed in agony; another he pushed to his death from a castle turret.

At around this time the scheming Oyamada Tamon invited the couple to a special entertainment at his house. Always eager to curry favor with his lord, he decorated his garden with human heads placed where they could be seen from the house, much to the delight of Tadanao and Ikkoku. He then had a pregnant woman brought out and beaten with a large mallet until she aborted the fetus, a display that afforded his guests great amusement.

In 1622, six years after Tanjuro had taken up his post, the same Tadanao demanded that Nagami Uemonnosuke give his mother to him as a mistress. Uemonnosuke's mother had remained celibate after her husband followed his lord in death by committing suicide, but she was a well-known beauty and, having had only one child, looked much younger than her thirty years. This was the event that led to the destruction of Tanjuro's dreams.

The sixteen-year-old Uemonnosuke refused and, summoning his retainers, made preparations to defend his home. Meanwhile, his mother shaved her head and entered a nunnery. When Uemonnosuke spied Tadanao climbing up to the second floor of a falconer's building, he shot at him with a large-bore musket but missed. Things remained stalemated until the New Year holidays, when Uemonnosuke sent his retainers home for the festivities and Tadanao seized the opportunity to attack. Realizing that further resistance was pointless, Uemonnosuke set fire to his house and committed ritual suicide.

Tanjuro had been in the thick of the fighting, but on hearing of his young master's suicide, he slipped through the smoke of the burning house, collected his wife and daughter, and set out on the road once more, the noise of the battle still echoing in his ears.

Tanjuro's search for a new master was proving to be a lengthy one. Five years had passed and a second daughter had been born. He had become accustomed to life on the road and no longer cared if people looked askance at his appearance. As long as his family had sufficient food, he was happy to sleep under any shelter that offered itself, just like a common vagrant. To earn enough to feed his family, he chopped firewood at inns where they stayed, or if he came across work being done on roads, he would take a job as a laborer.

Tanjuro was thinking that, provided they had food, they could get through the night somehow.

"I'm sorry," Tami said to him. "We had three rice balls left from lunch, but the girls and I each had one when we stopped on the hill before coming into town."

Tanjuro guessed they must have eaten them while he was asleep. Tami and the children looked thin enough, but they had surprising appetites. Even the younger girl, Ito, could eat as much as her sister, Matsue.

"Well, it can't be helped. Let's look for an inn," he said.

"What about money?

"I have a plan."

The family looked so wretched that no innkeeper would be blamed for turning them away at the door. This had happened frequently in the past, leaving them no alternative but to pay in advance. This time, however, they had no money. The only thing they possessed was the letter of recommendation to Tsugé Hachirozaemon, which gave proof of Tanjuro's identity. An innkeeper could not turn away someone who had business with the chamberlain, so once they managed to find a room they should be able to stay on until Tanjuro received a post. It was with this plan in mind that he had asked Tsugé's wife to return the letter to him.

"I knew you'd think of something," Tami said. She trusted him implicitly. Many times in their years on the road they had been almost penniless, but not once had Tanjuro let her or the children go hungry.

They asked for directions to the Tokiwaya inn that Tsugé's wife had suggested, but instead of approaching they stood a little distance away and regarded it in silence.

It was a grand building with an entrance hall as large as a rich samurai's residence. A stream of people was entering and leaving, some travelers among them, but none of them looked poor. Suddenly, a maid rushed out, her wooden clogs echoing on the flagstones, to light the lanterns suspended from the gateposts. The inn was obviously flourishing. Its name, written in large black script, stood out conspicuously on the paper lanterns in the darkening street.

"This will not do. Let's look for something smaller," Tanjuro said. He walked off into the night, the footsteps of his family close behind.

"Katayanagi Zusho? Of the Aizu domain?" Tsugé Hachirozaemon tilted his head in thought as his wife helped him out of his traveling clothes. "I can't think who it might be," he said, sitting down while his wife poured him tea.

Tsugé did not like mysteries, and if there was something he did not understand he would worry over it until he found an answer. His wife had told him about the man bearing the letter of recommendation who called while he was away, but for the life of him the chamberlain could not recall the writer of the letter. It was most vexing.

"Are you sure you've never met him?"
"Yes."

"But it seems odd that somebody should come all this way to see you with a letter from a stranger."

"It does, doesn't it?" He could not fathom it at all. Writing a letter like that implied that Katayanagi was a close acquaintance of his. Suddenly an old memory stirred in his mind. "Wait!"

"Have you remembered?"

"Just a minute."

He dredged up a faint recollection. But had that man been called Katayanagi? While he was stationed in Edo, he had once paid an official visit to the Hiraiwa clan. At that time the clan had been in charge of Fuchu province, and he seemed to remember that he had met someone there named Katayanagi. However, he had only met the man on two occasions, and that was more than twenty years ago.

"Hmm, it must be that Katayanagi," he said, sounding pleased with himself. He was surprised to learn that Katayanagi was now serving the Kato clan in Aizu and was recommending somebody to him.

"Do you remember now?"

"I think so, but it's nobody I know well. I only met him a couple of times, years ago." His interest now turned to the man Katayanagi was recommending.

"What was the man's name again?"

"Oguro Tanjuro."

"What kind of person is he?"

His wife lowered her face in order to hide a smile as she recalled her surprise at seeing the ragtag family crowded in the entrance hall.

"What's wrong?"

"Nothing," she said, looking up, her eyes dancing with merriment. "His clothes were in a terrible state."

"That's not what I asked," Tsugé scolded her. "I want to know what kind of man he is."

"He's thirty-five or thirty-six years old, very thin and serious-looking."

"Sounds quite ordinary."

"His wife is most beautiful."

"He has a wife?"

"Yes. And two children." She smiled once more at the memory of the clear-eyed girls.

"Strange," Tsugé said, crossing his arms as he thought. He could not understand why a man with a family should be visiting him. "You say he took the letter with him. But what did Katayanagi say in it?"

"That Oguro is looking for a post. He asked you to treat him favorably."

"A post?"

"Yes. Are you taking on retainers for the castle? Katayanagi wrote that you were."

"Nonsense!" Tsugé exclaimed. "That was finished long ago."

"Oh dear," his wife said, dismayed. "You mean you don't need more men?"

"No."

This Oguro family seemed rather absurd, he thought, like actors coming onstage to perform just as the final curtain was descending. It galled him to think that he was somehow involved in the farce. He felt annoyed, and his irritation was directed at

Katayanagi, a man he hardly knew, for putting him in this awkward predicament.

"It's the height of irresponsibility."

"But Oguro will be coming to see you tomorrow," his wife said. "At least meet him and hear what he has to say."

"I never said I wouldn't meet him."

The next day Tsugé returned from the castle to find Oguro Tanjuro waiting for him. Tanjuro could not suppress a smile as he greeted the chamberlain.

"I am Oguro Tanjuro. Your esteemed wife may have told you about me." Having said that, he thrust his hand into the front of his kimono and withdrew the letter, which he held out to Tsugé. "I have a letter from Katayanagi Zusho recommending me to you."

Before reading the letter, Tsugé scrutinized the man in front of him. His nose and forehead were darkened almost black from exposure to the sun, but his cheeks and chin were so pale that it was obvious he had just shaved off his beard. His sunken cheeks had the effect of highlighting the contrast, making the man look as if he was wearing the lightweight face guard favored by some men in battle. As Tsugé's wife had said, his clothing was a mass of darns, but it was clean.

He looked at the letter of recommendation.

> *I understand that your clan is at present looking for new men, and in this connection I would like to introduce an old acquaintance. He is a man of excellent character in all respects, and I hope that you will consider his application favorably . . .*

The letter went on to give a summary of Oguro's career, describing how, after the dissolution of the Hiraiwa clan, he had found a post with the Matsudaira clan.

He has a nerve, Tsugé thought as he felt his anger toward Katayanagi mounting and spilling over to encompass the shabby man with the two-toned face standing before him. He took exception to the man's ingenuous expression of happy expectation.

"I don't like to disappoint you," Tsugé said, clearing his throat, "but I'm afraid that while I do know Katayanagi Zusho, we are not sufficiently close for him to have sent me a recommendation of this kind."

Tanjuro watched him in silence, a puzzled look on his face.

"I met him on official business once or twice more than twenty years ago, when I was posted in Edo. That's the extent of our relationship."

Tanjuro looked blank.

"Do you understand? I spoke to him two or three times on official matters, that's all. We are not friends by any means. In fact, it took me a long time even to recall his name last night."

"That can't be!" Tanjuro exclaimed, his eyes widening in disbelief.

"Furthermore, the hiring of new people mentioned here," Tsugé continued, tapping the paper with the index finger of his right hand, "was completed last month. It's been over for almost a month now."

Tanjuro groaned and seemed to shrink before Tsugé's eyes.

"So all the posts have been filled and we will not need anyone for some time."

Now that Tsugé had said it, he felt a surge of pity for the ronin who had rushed all the way from Aizu with his family, only to have his hopes dashed.

It's so irresponsible of him! Tsugé thought, silently cursing Katayanagi.

"Are you close to Katayanagi?" he asked.

"Yes," Tanjuro replied distractedly. "He was a good friend of my father's."

"I see." Suddenly the whole situation became clear to Tsugé. "Were you staying with him long?"

Tanjuro counted on his clumsy, bony fingers.

"When I was a ronin the first time, we stayed with Katayanagi for three months. After the Hiraiwa clan was disbanded, he was fortunate in that he soon found a post with the Kato family. Then, after I left the Matsudaira clan, we stayed with him for six months. And this last time we were there for ten days."

"Was it Katayanagi who told you we were looking for people?"

"Yes."

So that was it! Katayanagi had just wanted to be rid of unwanted guests. It must have been hard for him to look after a family of four who had no prospect of work. That explained why he had taken advantage of their past meeting to send the family to him.

"What work does Katayanagi do in the Aizu clan?"

"He is in the construction corps."

"How large is his income?"

"Four hundred bushels of rice a year."

Tsugé realized how difficult it would be for him to support the son of his old friend on such a meager income. The fact that he had done so for three, then six months revealed his loyalty as a friend, but in the end he had had to give up.

"I'm sorry to have wasted your time. I will take my leave now," Tanjuro announced in a suddenly more formal tone.

"That is our present situation. I hope you will not think too badly of me."

Even as he spoke, however, Tsugé discovered that his feelings were changing. He had cursed Katayanagi for sending the man to him like this, but perhaps Katayanagi had been acting in good faith. He may have remembered Tsugé well and recommended Tanjuro in the belief that he could be trusted to be useful. If that were so, he could not dismiss this man and his family out of hand.

"Where will you go from here?"

"I've not thought about that yet," Tanjuro replied.

"Will you be going back to stay with Katayanagi?"

"No. That would be difficult." When they had left, Tanjuro remembered Katayanagi slipping him some money for travel expenses without telling his wife.

"Don't go just yet." Tsugé was impressed by the man's candor. He had nowhere to go, but he had not made any excuses for his plight or begged for help, and he had said goodbye without trying to linger. Tsugé suddenly felt that it would be a shame to lose such a man. "I'll ask around," he said, half to himself.

"I beg your pardon?"

"I don't want to raise your hopes, but since you have come such a long way, I would like to help."

Relief flooded into Tanjuro's face. He bowed low, pressing his forehead to the tatami floor. "I would be extremely grateful."

"Well, I assume you're in no hurry to go elsewhere. But please understand that I cannot promise anything."

"Thank you very much. Even if you cannot find anything, we will be no worse off than we are now. If worse comes to worst, we will leave without complaint."

"Do you have any other references?"

"Yes, I do." Tanjuro reached inside his kimono and took out his package of documents. "This is confirmation of my position and conduct with the Hiraiwa clan."

After scanning it, Tsugé said, "I see you had an income of 900 bushels."

"Yes. And this is a testimonial to my actions during the siege of Osaka Castle, together with a witness report."

"May 8, 1615. So you were fighting under the chancellor of the Matsudaira clan of Echizen? That must have been some battle." Tsugé paused to read the report. "You fought the enemy with spears and took one head." He glanced over at Tanjuro and saw that the man was flushed with pride at the memory.

"Just one head, that of a foot soldier . . ." Tsugé murmured and, leaving the witness report unread, returned the documents with a heavy heart. "Do you have any special expertise with weapons?" he asked, not very hopefully.

"Yes," Tanjuro replied brightly. "I have some skill with the short sword."

Repair work on the embankment of the Goken River finished at sunset, and by the time Tanjuro arrived back at the inn in Hatsuhana it was already too dark to see people's faces clearly. Before entering through the rear door, he washed his hands and feet at the well in the back garden. Light was spilling out from the kitchen as he passed by, and he heard the lively voices of women and the clatter of dishes being washed, but luckily nobody noticed him.

The smell of cooking rice reminded him how hungry he was, but just as he reached the stairway leading to the second floor, he came face to face with the landlord, Gonzo.

"Ah, landlord, this is good timing," he said, taking out his purse and placing some copper coins on Gonzo's large palm. "These are for our meals tomorrow," he said cheerfully.

The landlord accepted the money without a word and continued on his way.

What a rude man, Tanjuro thought, but considering he was paying only for their meals and nothing for the room, he was in no position to complain. As he forced his weary legs up the stairs, he looked out of the window and saw that the next day promised to be fine again. He was paid by the day as a laborer on the river works, and as long as it did not rain he could earn enough to feed his family. He walked along the corridor to the room at the end, which had been a storeroom until it was turned over to them. He opened the door and walked in.

"Welcome back," Tami said from the gloomy interior. "The children are already asleep, so be careful where you step."

He heard the sound of flint striking steel and a small standing lamp began to glow dimly. Tanjuro could see the girls asleep along the wall and a small table next to the lamp set with a meal. Oil was expensive, so the lamp was only used for the short period when he ate his meal. The children understood this, so as soon as dusk fell they would spread out their thin bedding and go to sleep.

"No word from Tsugé?" he asked, beginning his meager dinner of boiled barley and millet mixed with a handful of rice, and a dish of fern shoots and radish pickles.

"Not yet." Tami sounded worried. A month had passed since they first moved into this inn. They had trusted Tsugé to find Tanjuro a post, but there had been no word from him. Tanjuro considered going to inquire if there was any news, but he refrained, not wishing to appear importunate or to be a source of irritation to Tsugé. Moreover, he had to work so hard at the river for their daily food that by the time he came back and had eaten, all he wanted to do was sleep.

"Er . . ." Tami began hesitantly.

"What is it?"

"The landlord was here again demanding his money." Tanjuro was struggling to bite through the tough radish. "He wants us to pay for the room."

Tanjuro did not reply.

"He says otherwise we can't stay."

"Ignore him," Tanjuro retorted, after biting off a chunk of radish.

When they had arrived at the Kariganeya inn, the chief clerk had first talked to them, but the landlord, named Gonzo, soon took over. Gonzo read the letter addressed to Tsugé Hachirozaemon and studied the family for a few minutes before grudgingly agreeing to let them stay.

Ten days passed, and Gonzo asked to be paid for that period, but when he learned that the family had no money, his attitude changed completely. They were moved into the storeroom, and they received no more food or oil for the lamp. It was obvious that Gonzo was trying to force the family to leave, but after talking things over it was agreed that Tanjuro would pay for their meals in cash. That was how matters had stood until today. Tanjuro had explained that Tsugé was helping him look for a post, but Gonzo no longer believed him.

"He said that if we can't pay, I should sell my body and become a prostitute. He was quite rude."

At this Tanjuro laid down his chopsticks and sat with a dazed expression. Then his face turned bright red.

"How dare he!" He rose and, moving to the closet, took out his sword and thrust it in his sash.

"Where are you going?" Tami asked, getting up and blocking the door.

"I'm going to kill him. What he said is intolerable."

"Calm down! What good will killing him do? What would happen to the children and me? Is that why we came all this way?"

Tanjuro glared briefly at her, then put his sword back and sat down.

"I've eaten enough," he said and lay back on the worn tatami mats. "Tomorrow I'm going to sell my sword," he announced. When Tami returned after taking the dishes away, he was still lying on his back and staring at the ceiling.

Tami began to say something, but she thought better of it and let out a small sigh instead.

"Oh, I almost forgot," she exclaimed brightly. "Tora gave me a treat today. Please get up and try it."

Not everybody at the inn treated them like pariahs. One of the maids, a woman in her forties named Tora, would often slip them something good to eat. Hearing that it was food, Tanjuro sat up and watched as Tami placed ten walnuts in front of him.

"Can you crack them open for me?"

"Of course."

Rising, he again took out his sword, removed a small knife from its sheath in the scabbard, and used it to prize open the nuts. Tami wiped the tip of her hairpin and scooped out the nutmeat with it. A delicious fragrance filled the room.

The two of them concentrated on the walnuts until they were all eaten. While Tami picked up the shells, Tanjuro lay back on the floor again until she blew out the lamp shortly afterward. As soon as she did so, the silvery light of the moon flooded into the room through the open window, bringing with it a chilly night breeze. Tami lay down next to her husband.

"It's a beautiful moon."

"Hmm."

"It must be two years since we saw a moon like this. It was at Utsunomiya, do you remember?"

"Mmm."

"Stop that," Tami said, slapping his hand away. "We must make the bed and go to sleep."

Soon nothing more was heard but the sound of heavy breathing.

"Don't blame me if we have another child," she admonished, but her breaths began to come in gasps. Moonlight continued to stream into the room, and a lone cricket could be heard chirping mournfully in the darkness of the garden below.

Eventually they stopped moving, but Tanjuro remained lying on top of Tami. Soon his breathing slowed, and he began to snore gently.

Tami hugged him. "Poor man," she said. "Life is so hard for you."

The long-awaited messenger from Tsugé Hachirozaemon arrived in the evening of the first day of October. Tanjuro hurried back with him to Tsugé's house inside the castle.

"Some good news," Tsugé said. "A man has been sentenced to death, but our daimyo is a strong believer in martial spirit and has offered him the opportunity to redeem himself through trial by combat. When the chief councilor discussed it with me, I recommended that you be the one to carry it out."

Tanjuro remained silent.

"It's a marvelous opportunity," Tsugé said by way of encouragement. "If you are successful, you'll be offered a post immediately."

Tanjuro felt his body growing tense.

"Who is the man?"

"Someone named Yogo Zenemon. I don't think he will be hard to deal with."

It was during the recent induction of men into the clan that Yogo's skill at calligraphy had been recognized, and he had been given a post with the secretarial section. However, he had a perverse side to his character, which had led to frequent arguments with his colleagues. In a recent confrontation with a superior, he had made slanderous remarks about the daimyo, which was considered a form of treason and for this he had received the death sentence.

"What's wrong? You don't look enthusiastic. Do you wish to refuse?"

"No, I'll do it."

Tanjuro had been wondering what kind of person Yogo might be. Hearing that he was a newcomer made him feel somewhat reluctant, and he wondered if perhaps the man's perverseness had been acquired as a result of leading the hard life of a ronin. If so, he felt as if he were being asked to kill a man whose difficulties mirrored his own, almost like a friend. He wondered if the man had a wife and family.

"Yogo was hired with a stipend of 350 bushels of rice a year. If you're successful, I can guarantee you will receive no less."

"Three hundred and fifty!" Tanjuro's eyes flashed, and his sympathy for the man receded like an ebbing tide. "I guarantee that I will succeed."

"Be careful!" Tsugé called out as Tanjuro turned to leave. "He knows you're coming and that if he defeats you he will be pardoned. Yogo will be desperate, so be on your guard."

Tanjuro hurried through the darkened streets, guided to Yogo's house by Tsugé's servant. They passed through the brightly lit merchant district before entering the samurai quarter, which was calm and quiet in the moonlight.

"This is the house." The servant was a young man of about

twenty years of age, and as he spoke his voice trembled with apprehension.

"All right. You may go back now."

Tanjuro stood and watched the young man hurry off. Then he removed the cord attached to his scabbard and used it to tie up the sleeves of his kimono so they would not hinder his movements. He recalled the experience of facing arrows, spears, and swords in battle. The sensation was far from pleasant, but he forced down the horror and steeled himself.

The path to the house led between two tall hedges, and when he pushed the gate he found that it opened easily. Checking that no one was lurking on the other side, he stepped into the garden.

The front door of the house was open and a man was sitting on the step in front of the raised floor of the entrance hall. A candle burning behind him threw his face into shadow.

"So you've come for me then?" the man asked simply, and he suddenly rose to his feet. Tanjuro watched him warily.

"You'd better come in," the man continued.

With this, the man stepped up into the entrance hall and seemed about to enter the adjacent room, lifting the candlestick and affording Tanjuro a good look at his face. When he had heard that Yogo was a secretary, Tanjuro assumed the man would be small and plump, but he found himself facing a large, round-faced man of about thirty years of age.

Tanjuro moved inside the open doorway and stood in front of the raised floor of the entrance hall.

"Are you Yogo Zenemon?" he asked, to make sure it was the right man.

"That is correct," the man replied cheerfully. "I hope you won't be disappointed, but I intend to escape."

"Escape?"

"Yes. Will you let me go?"

"Why do you want to escape? This is trial by combat. If you win you will keep your position."

"I understand. But I'm not good at fighting and I doubt I can win." The man gave a nonchalant smile. "To tell the truth, I've had enough of the samurai life. I want to go back to my hometown and become a farmer."

"Where are you from?"

"Murakami in Echigo province. My family used to be powerful landowners. After the clan was disbanded, two or three of them returned to farming."

In 1618 the Murakami samurai mutinied against their daimyo, and when news of this reached the central government in Edo, the clan was broken up and its income of 450,000 bushels of rice confiscated. Apparently that was when Yogo had left the region, and ten years had passed since then.

"Were you a ronin the whole time after that?"

"Not exactly," was Yogo's vague reply. "I've held several posts, but none lasted very long. I was hoping this one would be different, but look what happened. I don't want to be a samurai any longer." Yogo sat down and stretched his legs out in front of him as if to demonstrate that he had no hostile intentions.

"So you intend to flee?"

As he listened to the man, Tanjuro let down his guard a little and noticed that Yogo was dressed in traveling clothes. He realized then that he could not kill the man. He would just have to tell Tsugé that Yogo had already fled when he arrived. He wondered how this would affect his chances of a post, although he still hoped he would be able to take over Yogo's. He could read and write, even if his calligraphy was not particularly attractive.

"May I sit down?" he asked.

"Please do."

"You're very lucky," Tanjuro said, sitting at the edge of the raised floor of the entrance hall. "If I owned some land, I'd never have come here."

"Have you been a ronin for long?"

Now it was Tanjuro's turn to talk, and he spoke of the long years he had spent in search of a post. Yogo was a good listener, offering comments here and there in the narrative and drawing out the entire story. Tanjuro relaxed as the two men traded confidences, and finally he abandoned his guard completely.

"And in the end I even had to sell my sword to pay for the inn," Tanjuro confessed. "By the way, are you married?"

"No."

"It's better not to be. It's difficult to look after a family when you don't have a post. Look, the only sword I have now is a bamboo one!" With that, he drew his long sword just far enough out of the scabbard to reveal the bamboo blade. However, instead of sympathizing with his plight, Yogo suddenly fell silent. Tanjuro looked up suspiciously and saw a strange gleam in Yogo's eyes. His face was twisted with evil delight as he stared at the bamboo sword.

"Well, that changes everything!" Yogo exclaimed, jumping to his feet and placing his hand on his sword hilt.

"Stop it! Don't be a fool!"

Tanjuro stood up just as Yogo's sword whistled through the air toward his head. He quickly drew his short sword and deflected the blade. He grazed his little finger as he did so, but there was little doubt about the final outcome. Keeping his short sword low, Tanjuro followed Yogo as the latter retreated further into the house. Beads of perspiration streamed down Yogo's face as he was forced on the defensive. Tanjuro had failed to mention that he was a master of the Toda School of short-sword fighting. He feinted to the left and, as Yogo moved to defend himself, drove his sword deep into the undefended right side of his opponent's body.

Tanjuro looked down at Yogo's lifeless body for a while before sheathing his sword. A samurai's lot is a wretched one, he thought. It was not the first time he had felt that way.

The old lord of Tanjuro's first clan had been one of the shogun's closest advisers, but this did not stop the government from disbanding the clan and confiscating its wealth immediately after his death. Then, at Tanjuro's next post, his master had tried to win greater glory for the clan but had ended up committing suicide, without a thought of what would happen to the men who followed him.

Samurai depended on their stipend of rice for survival and were helpless in the face of callous or suspicious masters. Yogo had not been immune to this fact of life, and Tanjuro believed that he really had intended to flee. When it came down to it, however, he had been unable to abandon the steady income his post provided. Even though his decision was the result of a misunderstanding, he had decided to fight rather than lose his 350 bushels of rice.

Tanjuro walked out through the garden gate to find a samurai and two servants with staves waiting on the moonlit street. Tsugé had obviously sent them to witness the result.

"Are you Oguro Tanjuro?"

Tanjuro nodded and pointed to the house where Yogo's body lay. After watching them enter the house, he untied the cord binding his sleeves.

At least we won't have to worry about tomorrow's meals, he thought. He pictured Tami and the children, and a wave of nostalgia suddenly swept over him for their days of freedom on the road in the wind and rain.

A Passing Shower

A lone burglar was sheltering under the eaves of a small shrine dedicated to Hachiman, the Shinto god of war. His name was Kakichi.

During the day, Kakichi was a knife sharpener by trade. Carrying a box of whetstones and files, he walked the streets of Edo, advertising his services in a singsong voice. He specialized in knives, scissors, and sickles, but he also aligned the teeth on saws, which was why he had the files. It was while plying his daytime trade that he would be on the lookout for houses to visit again under cover of darkness. However, this did not mean that he considered his job as a mere front for his nighttime activities. Kakichi was a hard worker and considered knife sharpening his real profession. The trouble was that every now and again a little devil inside his head would tempt him to break into someone's house. Whenever this occurred, he became utterly single-minded, and he was quite prepared to kill without the slightest compunction should someone try to raise the alarm. He had been living this double life for several years now but had yet to be surprised on the job.

It was raining hard. As Kakichi waited patiently for the shower to pass, he watched the raindrops hitting the ground and bouncing up again, glinting in the darkness. On the opposite side of the road was the tall black wooden fence surrounding a large secondhand goods store called Otsuya. Their wares all came from the city of Kyoto, and business seemed to be thriving.

When households utilized Kakichi's services during the day, he would be made to work outside, usually by the back door. While thus engaged, he had plenty of opportunity to case the house—going inside for a drink of water or to use the toilet—and in this way judge whether it would be easy to break into or not. If a place showed promise, he would drag out the work, eat his packed lunch in the kitchen, and get a general idea of the layout of the house, both inside and out. And while having his lunch he would chat and banter with the maids.

Kakichi was thirty-two years old, of average build, and was neither handsome nor ugly. In fact, his features could be described as nondescript. Even so, on learning that he was unmarried, quite a few female servants would immediately become more friendly. Years of experience had taught him to assess how secure a house was from the behavior of the servants working there.

He had been called to the Otsuya store twice before. As he was leaving the premises on this—the third—occasion, he tampered with the lock on the back gate to ensure it did not shut properly. A well-run household would send out for a carpenter to repair it at once, but Kakichi was betting that the Otsuya would not do that. He was banking on the store using some makeshift method to fasten the gate for the night. Even if he could not enter through the gate, though, he could climb over the fence.

All he had to do now was to wait for the rain to stop. It had started suddenly just as he arrived, but the night sky was beginning to lighten and take on a grayish tinge, so he guessed the shower would not last long.

There was not a soul about, no one whose suspicions might be aroused by the sight of a man lurking at the shrine. When he had arrived there, four or five people had been scurrying down the street trying to get home and out of the rain, but after that there was nothing but the steady beat of the rain on the street.

Suddenly he heard a voice and the sound of feet running into the shrine's small courtyard. Kakichi hurriedly slipped out of sight behind a corner of the building.

"Look at the time. What am I to do?" The voice was that of a young woman.

"Don't worry. Just say you had to shelter somewhere when it started to rain. My mother won't complain." This was a young man's voice. It was soft and smooth, and Kakichi supposed that it belonged to someone working in a store selling kimono or women's accessories, someone used to dealing with women customers.

"It's all your fault," the woman said accusingly. "When you suggested we meet, I thought you meant we'd go and have tea and then come back. I never dreamed you'd take me somewhere like that."

"You seemed happy enough to come," the young man replied with a chuckle.

"You make it difficult for a woman to refuse. But I'll never leave you now."

Then came a silence filled only with the sound of falling rain, and Kakichi could imagine the two embracing. From what he had heard, he assumed that the man was a store owner's son and the woman one of the servants. They had gone out on separate errands but had arranged for a rendezvous somewhere.

Damn them! I wish they'd hurry up and leave, Kakichi thought in disgust.

"What will we do now?" the woman asked languidly, sounding as though she were waking from a dream.

"I told you not to worry. I'll take care of everything."

"And you promise to marry me?"

"Yes."

"Oh, I'm so happy!"

They fell silent again, and Kakichi realized with irritation that they must be embracing once more. The rain began to slacken slightly.

"Just suppose . . ." the girl said in a wheedling tone.

"What?"

"Just suppose I became pregnant."

"Pregnant?" the man repeated, obviously shocked. Then, with a light laugh, he said, "You shouldn't try and scare me like that!"

"I'm not trying to scare you," the woman replied, her tone turning sharper. She was clearly a girl of some spirit. "It's quite possible, you know."

The man remained silent.

"It's been two months now."

"You're kidding." The man laughed again, but there was no humor in the sound. "You're just saying that to test me."

"No, I'm serious," the woman insisted. "I really might be pregnant. What are you going to do about it?"

"What am I going to do?" the man repeated, evidently at a loss. All trace of gentleness vanished from his voice. "You can't even say for sure that you are pregnant yet. We'll have to wait a bit longer."

"And then what? What if I am pregnant?"

The man said nothing.

"Will you tell the master and mistress about us?"

"Well, if it comes to that," the man said coldly, "I won't have any choice."

"You promise?"

There was no reply.

"If you don't say anything, I'll tell the mistress myself."

"All right, all right. We can talk about this later. Look at you, you're soaked through. We must get back. You go first, and I'll follow later."

"We'll still see each other?"

"Of course."

There was the sound of wooden clogs on the flagstones of the shrine courtyard as the girl passed into the street.

"She's got to be joking," the man muttered to himself. "If my father finds out, he'll disown me." Then, adopting a stagy voice, he continued, "Iseya Tokusaburo, you are making the biggest mistake of your life. Your haste betrays you." The line was clearly from a Kabuki play, which showed that the young man was a fan of the theater.

Silence finally returned to the shrine. Peering around the corner, Kakichi realized that the man must have set off after the girl.

Heaving a sigh of relief, he looked out at the rain. As he had foreseen, it was falling more lightly now. The raindrops were no longer rebounding so forcefully from the ground, and the sound was softer. He imagined it would soon cease altogether.

I'll go in as soon as it stops, he thought. He had already planned the route he would take. He would enter through the back door, pass through the kitchen, and go down the corridor. This would take him past the maids' room, so he would have to be careful not to make any noise. There were three maids; one went home each evening, but that still left the two who lived on the premises.

One maid was called Okiyo. When she had learned that he was unmarried, she had been all over him, plying him with tea and rice crackers. Being on the plump side, she was probably not a light sleeper. It was the other one who worried him, a widow in her fifties, sharp-eyed and thin, the type who would awaken at the slightest noise.

Walking down the corridor past the maids' room would bring him to the living room. Okiyo had told him that the store owner and his wife slept in the room next to this, but it was his guess that the day's earnings were kept in the living room. Once, on the pretext of using the restroom, he had ventured inside the house, and as he walked past the living room he had seen the owner and the chief clerk there with a cash box. The door of the cupboard beneath the household shrine had been open but the cupboard itself was empty, so he presumed that must be where they kept the cash box. The family's valuables were stored in a separate building, but the owner did not look the type who would bother going outside to lock up the day's takings there every evening. However, once when he was sharpening knives outside a house . . .

Kakichi was brought out of his reverie by two shadowy figures standing at the shrine gate and speaking in whispers. This time it was two men. Kakichi moved nearer to try to hear what they were saying, but their voices were too low. He watched them with mounting annoyance, willing them to be anywhere but there. Then one of them raised his voice.

"We're getting soaked here," he said, with a gesture toward the shrine. "Let's shelter over there."

Not again, thought Kakichi crossly, but there was something about the voice that made him prick up his ears. He did not recognize it, but it was the kind of voice that would chill the bravest man's heart, and he wondered who it belonged to.

"No, I'm going home," replied the other. This voice did not seem to be that of a law-abiding citizen either. It had a cold, evil ring. "There's nothing more to talk about, Mino."

"Yes, there is," the first man retorted with a mirthless chuckle. "I want my cut. That's the way I operate. I'm not going to stand idly by while somebody tries to squeeze me out of my due, I don't care who they might be. Let's finish this here and now."

"Haven't you been listening at all? Nobody made any money so nobody gets a cut."

"That's not what Také said."

"I don't care what Také said. I didn't make a penny so there's nothing for you. That's all there is to it."

"If that's how you're going to play it, I guess I'll just have to tell the boss."

"Tell the boss?"

"That's right. Tagaya went to the boss to complain that he'd been cheated in a game. The boss got rid of him, saying that his dice were all clean, but if I was to tell him the truth . . ."

"Shut it!" the other man said sharply. "You really are a fool. And what do you think would happen to you if you did?"

"I don't know," the man called Mino replied. "But if I find out how much Tagaya lost that night, I'll know what my cut should be."

"Don't do it, Mino," the other man said in a quiet, menacing tone. "If you do, we'll have to pay. Personally, I don't mind, but what about Sukezo? It will mean trouble for him."

"In that case I'll keep quiet. All you have to do is give me my cut."

"Are you threatening me?"

"What do you think?" Mino sneered. "I know what's going on. I know you took my share and spent it on that girl, Okimi, in the brothel near the fire-lookout tower. You don't think I'd have it out with you without checking first."

"Well done. I suppose you found that out all by yourself?" the man asked, suddenly adopting a gentler tone.

"Of course. If you try to cheat me out of my money, I'll have to tell the boss about the woman, too. I'm not the fool you take me for. Hey, what's your game?"

One of the figures leaped out into the street pursued by the other, who caught him from behind and held him. There was a short, sharp cry, and Kakichi saw the flash of a blade before the two collapsed to the ground. The men kept up a stream of curses as they fought like wild beasts, rolling across the street as they struggled.

It was still raining, so they must have gotten covered in mud, but they showed no sign of stopping. They obviously intended to fight it out to the end.

Finally, one of them managed to get astride the other. Raising his knife, he plunged it into his opponent's body. Then both men lay motionless. The man with the knife must have used his other hand to gag his opponent because there was no sound at all.

The man on top eventually rose to his feet. Kakichi could hear him panting as he looked down at his victim. Suddenly he turned and ran off into the darkness, leaving the body in the street. Kakichi had watched dispassionately while the men fought. After the victor had disappeared, he went to the gate of the shrine and peered into the dark street.

He must be dead, Kakichi thought. He felt no particular sympathy for the victim, only anger that his plans had been interrupted. He could hardly break into the Otsuya store with a body lying in the street outside. It was unlikely that anyone would pass by at night, but he could not afford the risk. If somebody stumbled across the body while he was on the job, the whole district would soon be in an uproar and men from the magistrate's office would be called in. If that happened, he'd never be able to concentrate on the work at hand.

There was a small stand of trees behind the shrine, and although it would not be easy, he decided he had no alternative but to drag the body and hide it there before starting work. He cursed his luck, but just as he was about to step into the street, the body gave a moan.

Damn it, he's still alive, thought Kakichi, and he stepped back into the shadows to watch as the man struggled to his feet. After falling down several times, the man finally managed to stand up and stagger off into the night. He looked as if he would fall at any moment, but he somehow retained his footing and tottered down the street.

"That's the way! Keep it up!" Kakichi muttered encouragingly. He did not care what happened to the man as long as he went somewhere else to die. On the nights of his break-ins, Kakichi had little time for pity.

The man finally disappeared from sight and Kakichi walked back into the shrine courtyard, grateful that there was nothing to stop him now. The rain had ceased, and he looked around cautiously to check that he was alone. Apart from a sudden flurry of raindrops from the cedar trees in front of the shrine, all was quiet. It was eleven o'clock, a time when all good citizens were in their beds and only the more disreputable members of society were out.

Taking a deep breath, Kakichi was just about to cross the street when he saw a light bobbing toward him from the left.

"What now?" he exclaimed in exasperation.

He hurried back to his hiding place by the shrine, but the light was approaching at a snail's pace, so slowly in fact that it made him want to stamp his feet in frustration: all these intrusions were taxing his nerves. As the light finally drew level with the shrine, he made a silent shout for whoever it was to disappear. As if his cry had been heard, the light suddenly stopped moving. Then, to make matters worse, a woman spoke.

"Ochié, let's rest here a while."

The voice sounded pitifully weak but was answered by the clear tones of a young girl asking if her mother was still in pain. Kakichi poked his head out to see a woman in her mid-twenties entering the shrine compound with a girl of six or seven. He was close to weeping with vexation.

Despite her disheveled hair, the woman seemed to be quite beautiful, but even by the dim light of her lantern he could see she was abnormally pale. Both she and the girl were dressed in cheap, worn clothes.

That's all I need—an invalid, he thought, pulling back his head. He wondered whether the mother was sick and had ventured out at this hour to buy medicine, taking the child along for company. He could hardly ask her to move on in her weakened state, so he resigned himself to waiting until they went.

"Shall I massage your shoulders?" the little girl asked. They must have sat down on the steps leading up to the shrine.

"Yes, please."

"I wish we had never gone to see Father," the girl said in a surprisingly adult tone. "It only made him angry, and that woman told him not to let us into the house."

"I didn't want to go," her mother replied distractedly, as if her thoughts were far away. She sounded depressed. "But we can't pay the rent and the landlord's going to throw us out. If I was feeling better, I could have done something, but I've been sick for so long I had no choice but to ask him for money."

"Why doesn't Father come home anymore? What's he doing in that house?"

"I don't know," the mother said listlessly. "I suppose he prefers that woman to me. Even though he has you, a lovely daughter, he's gone crazy over her."

"Won't he ever come home?"

"No, we won't be seeing him again."

What a bastard, Kakichi thought, cold rage building inside him. From what little he had heard, he had a good idea of the woman's predicament. The man had deserted his sick wife and his daughter to move in with a younger woman, leaving them threatened with eviction. As a last resort the woman had gone to beg him for money, only to be turned away empty-handed.

What a terrible shame, Kakichi thought, his anger almost making him speak out loud.

Kakichi had once had a wife called Oharu. At the time he had been employed in a smithy and had loved his work. Oharu was pregnant, and he was eagerly anticipating the birth of their child. Kakichi's employer valued him as a reliable worker and paid him well, so although their life was far from luxurious, he and his wife did not want for anything.

Kakichi was good at his job, and his boss had promised to set him up in his own business one day. Kakichi and Oharu liked to talk about the future, about where they should build their smithy and how they would need to hire two apprentices. But this happiness came to an abrupt end when Oharu died, taking her baby with her. At first they thought the cold she had caught would soon pass, but in her condition Oharu was not strong enough to fight it. The fever rose and she wasted away before his very eyes.

Kakichi had never been fond of alcohol, but after Oharu's death he began to drink heavily, with the result that he started taking time off work. He would not listen to his boss's advice and their relationship soured until one day he just walked out. After that he worked as a casual laborer, spending the day in bed when there was no work. Nothing in life had meaning anymore. He only worked to feed himself, and even doing that was an effort.

One day, while walking along a city street, Kakichi had passed a large house decorated with festive red-and-white-striped bunting, indicating that some kind of celebration was in progress. People were rushing in and out of the house, and occasional bursts of laughter could be heard in the street. As waves of laughter followed one after another, Kakichi was all at once seized by an uncontrollable rage.

What are they so happy about? he thought in disgust. He knew he was not being fair, but he could not stop the black anger that surged in his heart. If he was forced to explain it, he could only say that it was rage against the happiness in the world. The memory of his own short-lived joy had allowed him to keep going, but the sound of that laughter smashed whatever dreams he had left, exposing their lack of substance. The laughter appeared to be mocking him, saying, "This is true happiness."

He could not accept that there were happy people and sad people, and that those who were happy now would soon experience the opposite state, or that unhappy people would in time come to know joy. Instead, his heart was filled with hatred for everyone who was happy.

Later that night, when sleep had descended over the city, Kakichi roamed the streets like some nocturnal creature until he reached the house where he had heard the laughter. Creeping inside, he robbed them of all their money.

"Are you hungry, Ochié?"

"No."

"If you're hungry, just say so. It makes me sad to see you trying to be so good."

"In that case I am hungry."

"I thought so. Look at the time. When we get back, I'll borrow some rice from Osué and cook you some dinner."

Listening to them, Kakichi felt tears welling up in his eyes. It was as if he were listening to his own dead wife and child.

What a terrible shame, Kakichi thought again, cursing the woman's husband for deserting a good wife and daughter for another woman.

"Let's go then."

"Are you sure you can walk?"

"I'm all right. We've come a long way, haven't we? Ochié, can you take my hand like you did before?"

Kakichi heard them get to their feet. He peered cautiously around the corner of the shrine building. They were moving at a snail's pace, and the mother was obviously very weak.

Will they make it home? he worried, watching as they left the shrine compound and passed into the street. Just then the woman stumbled and fell to her knees. The girl started to cry.

"I knew it!" he cried, and leaped out of his hiding place.

The woman flinched at his sudden appearance. Clutching her daughter to her, she looked up at him, her eyes wide with fear. He saw he had been right and that she was extremely pretty.

"Don't be frightened," he said quickly. "I was sheltering from the rain in the shrine and didn't show myself when you arrived.

Sorry if I scared you." He helped the woman to her feet. Noticing the child staring at him, he ruffled her hair. "My name's Kakichi. I'm a knife sharpener from Motomachi in Fukagawa. I'm a respectable man so don't be alarmed. Where are you heading?"

"Tomikawa in Fukagawa."

"Then we're almost neighbors," he replied brightly. "I'll see you home. It will take you the whole night at this rate."

"Please don't bother," the woman replied, regarding him suspiciously. Kakichi realized that the black scarf he had wrapped around his head was obscuring part of his face and contributing to her distrust of him. He hurriedly removed it.

"No need to stand on ceremony."

"Please don't worry. You carry on. We'll go slowly at our own pace."

"If you're sure . . ."

Kakichi stood and watched the two set off, but hardly had they started to walk when the mother staggered and collapsed on her knees once more. Still holding her mother's hand, the young girl turned and looked back at him in silence.

Kakichi hurried to where the woman was kneeling, trying to catch her breath. He crouched down and offered her his back. She seemed to have exhausted her last reserves of strength and, after a moment's hesitation, she leaned against him. He rose to his feet, lifting her on his back.

"It was wrong of me, I know, but I overheard what you said," Kakichi admitted as he carried her over Mitsume Bridge. "I'm only a poor knife sharpener, but I would be happy to help you." As he said this, she abandoned all her defenses and he felt her body relax. She did not say anything, but he was content that she no longer feared him. He gently hitched her higher on his back.

Carrying the woman and holding the girl's hand, Kakichi walked through the dark streets guided by the feeble glow of the woman's lantern. He felt as if he had done this before, sometime in the distant past. It was hard to believe that just a short while ago he had been preparing to break into the Otsuya store.

The weather had cleared up now, and stars began to appear one after the other in the night sky.

All for a Melon

"A woman is impossible to control once she's past thirty," Kusaka Jinnai remarked suddenly.

Here we go again, thought Hankuro. From experience he knew that whenever Jinnai threw out a comment like this, it meant only one thing: he was having another fight with his wife. He made the remark sound like a general observation, but from the bitterness in his tone it was obvious he had someone particular in mind, namely, his wife.

Hankuro knew that Jinnai was cursed with a troublesome spouse. He had never met her but had heard so much about her from Jinnai over the years that her reputation was firmly fixed in his mind. And she didn't sound so different from his own wife, Misa, who was not a good spouse either. He had never complained about her to Jinnai, although he had been on the verge of doing so once, but then Jinnai had begun harping on his own wife's faults and had continued for the whole evening. So Hankuro missed his chance and had been forced into the role of sympathetic listener ever since.

"Not at it again, are you?" Hankuro asked casually. Having heard his friend's grievances so many times, he knew exactly how to handle him. The trick was to stay aloof, yet show an occasional willingness to listen. "It can't be as bad as you think. Every couple squabbles some time or other."

Both men worked in the domain's construction corps and studied the art of sword fighting together at the Torii dojo, so Hankuro was prepared to hear Jinnai out for the sake of their long friendship. This time, however, Jinnai did not seem pleased with Hankuro's response and threw him a sharp glance.

"She hasn't spoken to me for three days," he said glumly.

"Oh?" Hankuro replied in a noncommittal tone.

"Three days! What kind of woman would do that?" Just talking about it was enough to rekindle Jinnai's ire. He broke off, lost for words, but Hankuro was not overly impressed by the revelation. He only had to go home to find another woman just like her, as Misa had not spoken to him for the past two days either.

It was all because of the ceremony to mark the third anniversary of Hankuro's mother's death, which was coming up in a month's time. Misa had been pestering him to buy her a new kimono for the occasion, and finally he had lost his temper, making her retreat into silence. But that was not the end of it. Her face had remained pale and tense, and occasionally he would catch her glaring at him like a snake eyeing its prey. And she refused to speak another word. To make matters worse, their daughter, Fumi, took her mother's side and also shot angry glances at him. The atmosphere in the house was icy, to say the least.

"What about a drink?" Hankuro suggested when they reached the corner at Teppo, where they usually parted.

Jinnai stood with his arms crossed as though trying to decide, but Hankuro was not fooled. Hankuro liked a drink now and then, but Jinnai loved his saké, and despite his slight build he could down large quantities without any apparent ill effect. He was putting on a show of hesitation to dispel any suspicion that he might have brought up the subject of his domestic spat as an excuse to go drinking. But his feet were already pointing toward Mishima, an area filled with drinking houses.

"There's no point in going home if you and your wife are just going to sit and stare at each other. Don't worry about the bill. I don't have any cash on me, but I run a tab at the Imoriya. A drink's the best medicine at times like this," Hankuro urged.

"True enough. You can't beat a drink."

Jinnai's mood suddenly brightened as he led the way through a maze of streets to Mishima. Samurai were not supposed to be seen drinking in public after work, and edicts had occasionally been issued by clan officials forbidding the practice, but these were never effective for long.

"Who do they think they are?" drinkers would exclaim indignantly. "The officers are forever going to high-priced establishments at public expense, so what's wrong with us having a drink if we're prepared to pay for it?" In no time the narrow streets of Mishima would once more be filled with tipsy samurai—Jinnai and Hankuro among them.

From outside the Imoriya looked small because of its narrow frontage, but the tavern stretched back a considerable distance, with a corridor running all the way down the center. To the left was a raised platform with small rooms on it, and to the right was a long table with seats fashioned from old barrels. The rooms on the left had no doors, but custom dictated that they were reserved for samurai, while farmers and townsmen sat at the table. There were no windows in the Imoriya—the only light came in through the entrance and from a skylight in the kitchen at the far end—so it was quite dark even in daylight hours. As customers arrived, the staff would place lamps on the floor beside them or light the hanging lanterns.

They sat down in one of the rooms, ordering saké and a few accompanying dishes. As soon as the saké arrived Jinnai cheered up visibly and began flirting with the waitress, Osome, whom he knew from previous visits.

"A drink's the best medicine at times like this, right, Hankuro?" he said, repeating his friend's words and holding out his cup to be filled. Hankuro was not really in the mood to listen to Jinnai's problems, but he felt obliged to help him let off steam.

"So what started it?" he asked after taking a few sips.

"What started what?" Jinnai had been so absorbed in making a mental tally of the attributes of the five waitresses that he looked momentarily puzzled by the question.

"The fight with your wife that's resulted in her not speaking to you for three days," Hankuro said patiently.

"Oh, that." Brought back to reality, Jinnai sighed heavily. "It was about our son."

Jinnai was thirty-three years old, four years older than Hankuro. He had married when he was twenty-one, and his first son was born the following year. Jinnai began finding fault with his wife five or six years ago, although that did not stop them having three more children during that time. Including the two they already had, that made a total of five children. This might seem a lot for an incompatible couple, but Hankuro understood the reason. Some people ended up having children as a result of their squabbles, although Jinnai was doubly unfortunate in that it was his children who were often the cause of the arguments. It was a vicious circle from which there was no escape.

The latest fight had been about their second son, who had just turned seven—whether to send him to the clan school or to the sword fighting dojo in town.

"I said that book knowledge and the arts are fine for girls, but a boy has to learn sword fighting."

"I agree with that."

"So what do you think my wife said?"

"No idea. What did she say?"

"That with no more wars, sword fighting was now a waste of time! What does she know? Even so, I could put up with that, but it was what she said next that really made my blood boil."

"What was that?"

"She said I only have to look at myself to see that she's right. The gall of that woman!"

Hankuro and Jinnai had been studying at the Torii dojo for two decades now. Since the age of twenty, they—together with Tomono Zensuke of the infantry corps—had been recognized as the best students in the dojo. When they took part in contests against the rival Tatekawa dojo, which was popular among higher-ranking samurai, they were invariably the winners.

Their teacher, Torii Yazaemon, was getting on in years, so now it was Hankuro, Jinnai, and Tomono Zensuke who taught the students. The construction corps consisted mainly of lower-ranking samurai: Hankuro himself had a yearly stipend of 175 bushels of rice, Jinnai 90, and Tomono Zensuke, being in the infantry, received barely enough to feed himself, putting him at the bottom of the samurai hierarchy.

Despite this difference in salary and rank, Hankuro never acted condescendingly toward Tomono. Hankuro might be the more accomplished swordsman, but nobody could match Tomono for his thrusting technique, and quite a few times one of Tomono's thrusts would penetrate his guard. For Hankuro, the enjoyment he derived from sword fighting more than compensated for his lowly social status, and the same could be said of Jinnai and Tomono. The three were not often at the dojo at the same time, but when they did meet they would practice for hours, working up a sweat until late at night. Once, when Jinnai could not find a suitable parry for one of Tomono's thrusts, Hankuro had acted as referee and stayed with them while they practiced until it was almost dawn.

So Hankuro naturally understood Jinnai's indignation at his wife's remark. Jinnai was a gifted swordsman and his defense was virtually impregnable. He could hold off his opponent until he detected the slightest loss of rhythm that would give him the chance to attack. The reason Hankuro was the better swordsman was because his technique combined both attack and defense, whereas Jinnai concentrated solely on defense. Hankuro's more varied style enabled him to wait until Jinnai tired before moving in for the finish.

Although Jinnai was not able to defeat Hankuro, he was proud of his skill and the fact that no one else in the clan could penetrate his defense. However, his wife did not see things in the same light. To her, his skill in sword fighting did not count for much, and, more importantly, it did not lead to promotion.

"Well, I can understand why you're so upset."

"I knew you would. The truth is . . ."

Jinnai's voice trailed off and, looking up, Hankuro saw tears on his face. Jinnai would often weep when he was in his cups, although this did not affect the pace of his drinking.

"I feel so wretched."

"Don't worry. Have another one." Hankuro refilled Jinnai's cup.

"I knew you'd understand. You're a real friend," Jinnai said, sniffing. He had large eyes, prominent cheekbones, and sunken cheeks. His gaunt collarbone contributed to his general air of impoverishment. Tears caught in the sparse stubble on his cheeks glistened in the lamplight.

Hankuro sympathized with Jinnai's plight, but he felt it was time they went home. Once Jinnai entered his weepy phase he would begin drinking in earnest and never stop talking. Hankuro had offered to pay for the evening, and he did not want to spend more than he had to.

"The trouble with women is they don't understand what we men have to go through," he said.

"That's exactly the problem," Jinnai replied, emptying his saké cup and pouring himself another.

"Women should be pitied. The only way they can judge a man is by his income. They're incapable of recognizing a man's true worth."

"Yes, that's just it," Jinnai said, with another sniff. He was having trouble picking up some tofu with his chopsticks.

Hankuro parted company with Jinnai at the corner of Teppo and turned left toward his home in Samukawa. A pale moon lit the way, and when he looked up, he saw two rings around it, the inner one tinted with all the colors of the rainbow.

Hankuro was a little tipsy, but not enough for his walking to be affected. Actually he was feeling good, because while he and Jinnai had been criticizing women he had been able to forget about the argument with his own wife.

Hankuro knew that the root of the problem with Misa was money—or rather, the lack of it. That was what made her and Jinnai's wife behave as they did. In their day-to-day living, their poverty did not trouble them, but when the extended family gathered for funerals or weddings, their financial constraints were brought home to them. One of his relatives held the post of lieutenant, which commanded a grand income of 2,400 bushels of rice, and although Misa had no hope of competing with that, she at least wanted to be able to dress appropriately on family occasions. Unlike the wives of foot soldiers, who could grumble about their husbands in public, her social position did not allow her to do that. Instead she would just look daggers at Hankuro in the house and refuse to speak to him.

Even so, Hankuro could not spend money he did not have. He realized that Jinnai, with so many mouths to feed, must be in a far worse situation, and he worried about the reception his friend would face that evening when he arrived home in the condition he was in. If Jinnai walked in drunk, it would surely lead to another fight.

The road he was walking along was bordered on one side by the garden of Honda Sagami's mansion, enclosed by a white plaster wall topped with tiles. Honda was one of the domain's councilors, responsible not only for the pages and the musketeer corps but also for the construction corps led by Lieutenant Hosoda Shichibei. That made Honda his and Jinnai's commander, although Hankuro rarely saw him except on New Year's day, when he went to make his obeisances to Honda in place of the daimyo. Being a lower-ranked samurai, Hankuro was not permitted to approach the daimyo directly, so he prostrated himself in front of Honda instead. From these annual rituals he knew that Honda was a small man with white hair and a dignified manner, but that was the extent of his knowledge.

This was only to be expected, for Honda's elevated position put him far beyond Hankuro's orbit. In fact, Honda—with Chief Councilor Misaka Sadayu and his counterpart in Edo, Sugé Hannojo—was in charge of the administration of the whole domain.

Vaguely aware that it was Councilor Honda's estate he was passing, Hankuro was only aroused from his reverie when he heard the clash of swords. Breaking into a run, he turned the corner into a street behind the Honda residence to find two people—one of them a woman—facing each other with swords drawn. A blade flashed in the moonlight and the next instant the woman fell to the ground as though her feet had been swept from beneath her.

"Oh no, not another domestic squabble!" With all the women troubles he and Jinnai had been talking about, Hankuro's head was still in turmoil, and for a moment this seemed a likely explanation. Then his mind cleared. It was hardly conceivable for a married couple to take up swords and fight in the street.

"Stop!" he cried. The man, who was crouching down to search the woman, looked up in surprise and jumped to his feet. He stood in front of the body as though to hide it and waited in silence for Hankuro to approach, his sword still in his left hand. He appeared young, about twenty-five or twenty-six, but as far as Hankuro could tell in the dim moonlight he had never seen him before.

Hankuro studied his opponent's reactions carefully. The man did not say anything, but neither did he show any inclination to flee. He resembled a wild animal that had caught its prey and was not prepared to be deprived of it.

"Are you a common thief," Hankuro asked, "or do you have grudge against this woman?"

"Better not stick your nose into what doesn't concern you," the man replied with disconcerting arrogance.

Hankuro felt his anger rising. He might find his wife's recalcitrance annoying, but this man's attitude was far worse.

"When people take that tone, it merely increases my curiosity. You can't expect me to ignore what I've just seen."

"Do you intend to try and stop me?"

"Yes. I saw you searching the woman just now. As you haven't answered my question, I can only assume that you're nothing but a common thief."

"You'll regret this."

"That remains to be seen."

The man took a step back then suddenly lunged, his sword swinging down in a death stroke. Dodging to one side, Hankuro quickly moved backward, drawing his sword as he did so. Seeing Hankuro take a defensive pose, the man paused a moment and altered his stance. He was obviously no stranger to the art of sword fighting.

Hankuro could tell from the man's stance that he had studied at the Tatekawa dojo. The tip of his sword was aimed a little above eye-level, which was characteristic of that school. As he had already suspected from the man's haughty tone, this indicated that he must belong to one of the more powerful families in the domain.

Letting out a loud yell, the man attacked with a well-executed stroke, although his footwork left something to be desired. Hankuro ducked under the sword tip and parried, then moved onto the offensive, aiming for his opponent's arm. He had no wish to kill the man and only wanted to find out why an upper-class samurai would stoop to searching the body of a fallen woman like a common criminal.

The man swung his sword down over Hankuro's head, but Hankuro's sword was quicker and sliced into his opponent's right arm. The man raised his sword again and stopped abruptly, clutching his right arm with his left hand. He seemed to have lost all enthusiasm for fighting.

"Want to continue?" Hankuro inquired.

"No," the man replied, shaking his head. "You're a skilled swordsman. What's your name?"

"Not one you'll have heard."

"Humph!" The man moved back a few steps, still clutching his injured arm. "I'm warning you. If you help that woman, nothing good will come of it."

"I'll be the judge of that."

The man stared at Hankuro for a few moments, then turned and ran off.

Hankuro rushed to the woman's side. She had fallen facedown, her head to one side and her eyes closed, but as Hankuro approached, her eyes flew open and she tried to rise to her feet. She looked very young and was dressed in traveling clothes. Groaning with pain, she hoisted herself up on her left elbow and raised the dagger in her right hand to defend herself.

"Don't be alarmed. I'm not an enemy," Hankuro said quickly. "I'm here to help."

He could see her strength ebbing, and she collapsed to the ground once more, groaning.

Raising her to a sitting position, Hankuro checked her injuries. The sleeve of her kimono was ripped and there were two cuts on her left arm, but it had been the slash to her right shoulder that had felled her. It was a nasty wound, and the front of her kimono was soaked with blood.

Hankuro frowned. From her injuries he could tell that this samurai woman had put up a valiant struggle against an opponent who had attacked viciously, making no allowance for her sex.

"I'll soon take care of your wounds," he said, bending down and lifting the woman onto his back. As he set off with his soft burden, he realized he may have taken on a problem he could have done without.

"You'll regret this." The swordsman's words echoed in his ears. However, that was not what brought him to a sudden halt. He already had enough trouble with Misa, and he dreaded to think what she would say when he turned up with an injured woman on his back. But this was no time to worry about that, so he hurried on with the woman's groans continuing in his ear.

As Hankuro arrived at the front door, he found Misa looking sullen, obviously still angry from their argument.

"I have a wounded person here. Quick, make up a bed!" Hankuro snapped.

Misa's eyes widened in surprise, but the smell of blood and the injured woman's moans were enough to make her realize this was an emergency. She rushed into the back room to do as he had ordered. Driven out of that room, their daughter, Fumi, stood looking at her father in bewilderment.

"Don't just stand there. Go and boil some water!"

Hankuro watched with satisfaction as the ten-year-old fled into the kitchen. The plan he had devised as he trudged home with the injured woman on his back was proceeding smoothly. He had managed to get Misa and Fumi involved without giving them a chance to complain.

With Misa's help he laid the woman down on the thick quilts.

She grimaced, and another groan escaped her lips.

"What happened?" Misa asked, quickly removing the woman's straw sandals and undoing her leggings, all memory of their argument forgotten.

"I'm not sure," Hankuro said as he checked the wounds on the woman's arms and loosened the broad sash around her waist. "Somebody cut her down and was searching her when I came along, but I don't think it was an ordinary robbery."

Hankuro pulled open the collar of her kimono to inspect the wound on her shoulder. It was deep, cutting through the shoulder as far as the collarbone. Probing gently with his fingers, he found that the bone was not broken.

"First we must stop the bleeding. We need a doctor as soon as possible."

He told Misa to staunch the blood with the strips of cloth she had prepared. As he rose, he noticed that he had unintentionally exposed one of the woman's white breasts. But that was not what caught his attention. Hidden beneath her clothes next to her skin was a package wrapped in oiled paper. He knelt down once more and tried to remove it, but as he did so the woman's eyes opened and she seized his wrist. Her breathing was coming in short gasps, and her expression was one of despair.

"Don't worry," Misa said, leaning over her and looking her in the eye. "You have nothing to fear. This is the house of Shimada Hankuro of the construction corps. He rescued you and brought you here. We are tending to your wounds now, so don't be alarmed. My husband is an expert swordsman. Leave everything to him and it will be all right."

Hankuro was somewhat embarrassed to hear these compliments from Misa, but they seemed to have the desired effect on the woman. Either that or the exertion of seizing his wrist had used up her last reserves of strength, for she let go of his hand, closed her eyes, and resumed groaning.

So this is what he was after, Hankuro thought.

As he removed the package from the woman's clothing, his thoughts returned to the attack he had interrupted. The package was thin and obviously contained a missive of some sort. The outer covering was wet with perspiration, and when Hankuro opened it, he found a single sheet of paper. Kneeling beside the lamp he slowly read the contents, then raised it reverently above his head and bowed before folding it and rewrapping it in the oiled paper.

"What is it?" Misa whispered.

"Something of great importance," Hankuro said hesitantly. "It's a personal letter from the daimyo."

On hearing this, the color drained from Misa's face. Although she did not know what the letter said, she understood the seriousness of the situation. The bearer of a secret missive from the daimyo, Samanokami Toshitsuna, had been cut down and the letter would surely have been stolen were it not for Hankuro.

"We must not let anyone know she's here," Hankuro said. "I was going to fetch Doctor Ryoan, but this alters everything. Ryoan is useless when it comes to keeping a secret, so I'll go for Doctor Gido, even if he is farther away."

"That's a good idea."

"Don't let anyone in while I'm away. If someone tries to

force their way in, you will have to stop them."

"I will. Don't worry about us," Misa replied, her face ashen.

Misa was no beauty, and when they were married many of Hankuro's female relatives had remarked on this, implying that Hankuro was too good for her. But looking at her now, Hankuro thought her truly beautiful. As he left the house, he heard her calling for Fumi to come quickly.

Hankuro rushed out into the night. When he reached Gido's house, the doctor was already asleep, but on hearing what Hankuro had to say he hurriedly made ready to leave. Gido was an expert at setting bones and treating sword injuries. Whenever someone at the Torii dojo was injured, it was always Gido who was called in. He was a large man, and his brother, Kurosaka Sukenojo, was chief of the guards.

When they were halfway to Hankuro's home, Gido suddenly stopped.

"This isn't the quickest way to your house."

"No, but this is the route we have to take. If you turn left ahead, you'll come to Samukawa. Do you know where my house is?"

"Yes. I came when your daughter had an upset stomach. Once I visit a place, I never forget it."

"In that case, would you mind going alone? There's something I must do first. I won't be long."

Hankuro and the doctor parted at the corner of Yayoi, near Teppo, and Hankuro watched to make sure the doctor did not take the shortcut. Then he walked through Teppo toward Honda's estate. He had sent Gido the other way because he did not want the doctor to be seen in the area carrying his medical bag.

Hankuro edged cautiously up to the main gate of the estate but did not sense anyone's presence nearby. He continued creeping along the wall until he came to the corner. Stopping, he peered around it. The street was brightly lit by the moon, and he was able to make out several figures hiding by the wall opposite the rear gate of the Honda residence. Hankuro could not see exactly how many there were, but it seemed to be ten or more.

"Has anyone turned up yet?"

Hankuro almost jumped out of his skin, for the voice had come from close behind him. He had no idea how the man had got there.

"No, not yet," he whispered without turning around.

"What do you make of Okubo's story? Don't you find it a bit strange?" The man behind him clicked his tongue in disgust. "He says that the messenger from Edo is a woman, but who would trust a woman with something so important. I don't believe the enemy would be that stupid."

Enemy? Hankuro was shocked by the word. There must be a conspiracy afoot, something that a lower-ranking samurai like himself would not be privy to. Even though he could make no sense of the daimyo's letter to Councilor Honda, he knew it must be of vital significance. His chance encounter with the woman had thrown him into the eye of a storm.

"He said someone came along before he could finish her off, but I wonder if that was just an excuse for losing her. They say that whoever rescued her will definitely be back. What do you think?"

"Seems unlikely to me. We might as well all go back to bed," said Hankuro as he turned around.

The sight of Hankuro's face so shocked the man that he was speechless. "Who—?" Before he could finish the question, Hankuro dealt him a powerful blow and he slid unconscious to the ground.

It's pointless to try and deliver the letter tonight, Hankuro thought as he sped through the deserted streets. Councilor Honda was probably waiting for it, but the man Hankuro had struck down would have been discovered by now and the watchers would redouble their efforts. No, it was better to wait until the next day. With that decision, a heavy weight lifted from his shoulders and he slowed his pace to a walk.

But why should a letter from the daimyo have to be delivered in secret? Hankuro guessed that there must be some crisis in the domain, although he had no idea what it could be. He realized he would have to think carefully before making his next move. He would have to talk to the woman and find out what was going on.

The young woman regained consciousness at about six o'clock the following morning. Hankuro was debating whether to report for work or feign illness and take the day off, when Fumi called out excitedly to say she was awake.

The girl's face still looked flushed and feverish, and her eyes were misty and moist. She was very pretty, although the cast of her features hinted at a fiery temperament.

The doctor's expression had not changed when he saw the nature of the patient's injuries, and Hankuro was relieved he had asked Gido instead of Ryoan, their local physician, who was good but was also inquisitive and an inveterate gossip. If he were treating somebody with multiple sword wounds, he would not have been satisfied until he had heard the entire story.

Once Gido had finished cleaning and bandaging the woman's wounds, he told Hankuro that she had a fever but her life was not in danger. Then, lowering his voice, he said, "The muscles in her right shoulder have been severed, so she'll probably never be able to use the arm again."

She looked a mere eighteen or nineteen years old, and it would be a terrible disability for someone so young. Hankuro and Misa exchanged glances of sympathy.

"But at least she's not going to die," was Gido's brief comment.

As the doctor was leaving, Hankuro took him aside and asked him to return home the same way he had come, and not to breathe a word about this to anybody. As he did so, he realized he was involving himself in a conflict that he himself did not understand. On top of that, he had also involved Misa, for she had stayed up all night bathing the girl's forehead to try and bring the fever down. At dawn she woke Fumi to take her place and promptly fell into a deep sleep.

"How are you feeling?" Hankuro asked the young woman as gently as he could, kneeling beside her.

"Much better, thank you," she replied weakly, before breaking into a fit of coughing and grimacing with pain. "Where am I?"

She had obviously forgotten what Misa had told her the previous evening. However, she must know that she had been brought here after being injured in the fight in the street. She could not conceal her agitation.

"I am Shimada Hankuro of the construction corps, and you are in Samukawa. I brought you here last night to look after you. According to the doctor, your wounds are not fatal, so there's no need to worry. Just rest and take your time to recover."

Instead of looking relieved, she stared at him in silence. It shocked Hankuro to see that she still did not trust him.

"Don't be concerned about the letter," he said softly and smiled. "The man last night was trying to steal it, but I stopped him. However, I'm afraid that I have read it."

"Where is it now?"

"I have it in a safe place. You were trying to deliver it to Councilor Honda, so I thought I'd do that for you."

"Don't go in daylight. They're watching everybody who enters the estate during the day. Nobody must know that the letter has been delivered to the councilor." The woman became so distraught that her breaths started to come in shallow gasps. "If anybody finds out, his life will be in danger."

"They're watching Honda's residence at night, too." As Hankuro said that, it dawned on him that he could not visit the estate openly since he had fought with the man on guard the previous evening. He had to go unobserved, which meant going at night. That was the reason the woman had been there at that hour.

"I understand. I'll deliver the letter late tonight."

"Thank you. And please be careful." With that, her eyes lost focus and she lay back exhausted.

"Are you in pain?"

"Yes."

"What's your name?"

"Oriye."

She told him she was one of the ladies-in-waiting to the daimyo's wife in Edo. Her father worked under the chamberlain, but her mother and sisters lived in nearby Byobu.

"You must want to see them, but you'll have to wait a little longer. I will contact them as soon as I can."

He was amazed at the way he was adapting to the situation. Oriye made no reply. When he looked at her, he saw that she had fallen asleep. The fever, combined with her exhaustion from the long journey, was taking its toll. She may have acted like a mature woman, but her features still retained the softness of youth.

Fumi tiptoed into the room, and Hankuro motioned to her to continue bathing Oriye's forehead. He stood up and, although he was already a little late, prepared to report for duty in the castle.

Hankuro was apprehensive the whole day. He was usually paired with Jinnai, but his friend was called out twice to assist in surveying work for a new barracks by the main road and they had no time to meet. When the drum finally sounded in the evening, signaling the end of his shift, he hurried out of the castle. Jinnai, who had just returned from his assignment, came running up behind him.

"How are things with your wife?" Hankuro asked.

"Not so good," Jinnai replied with a scowl. "When I got home last night she knew right away that I was drunk and barred the door."

"What did you do?"

"I just lifted the whole thing off its runners. Women can be so childish sometimes."

Hankuro laughed when he recalled how serious Jinnai's problem had seemed the night before. The reason Jinnai could devote so much energy to feuding with his wife was simply that he had nothing more important on his mind. As for himself, not only was there an injured woman in his house but he also had the risky business of delivering the letter that night. All this had completely driven the argument with Misa from his mind.

"Do you fancy a quick drink?" Jinnai asked, nodding in the direction of Mishima as they turned the corner at Teppo.

"No, not today." Hankuro replied quickly. "You know, you should try being nice to your wife. I know she's not talking to you, but I'm sure she only wants a kind word from you. It's time you stopped quarreling and discussed your differences. Discussion, that's the key."

Having said that, he turned the corner and headed home, leaving Jinnai speechless.

As Hankuro approached the Honda residence, he saw that Oriye had been right. Two samurai were standing at the corner talking. They turned away when they saw him approach but did not leave their post.

The councilor's house was under observation.

The sky had been overcast since noon, and the clouds had become thicker as night fell. That made it easier for Hankuro to slip into the councilor's estate without being seen.

He walked on slowly in the darkness, wondering who could be

organizing the surveillance. He had asked Oriye, but she would not tell, saying it was not her place to explain. He knew the names of all the people responsible for the domain's administration. There was Chief Councilor Misaka Sadayu, Councilor Honda Sagami, District Steward Kumagai Heisuke in charge of agricultural affairs, Chief Councilor Sugé Hannojo representing the clan in Edo, and Chamberlain Ozeki Sahei. He had not heard of any conflict among them, but a major crisis must have developed while he and Jinnai had been preoccupied with their domestic squabbles.

The road from his home in Samukawa to Teppo climbed a gentle incline. Samukawa was where lower-ranked samurai and merchants had their houses, while Teppo was entirely given over to large samurai residences. The two districts were separated by a strip of land originally intended as a firebreak but which had overgrown with wild chrysanthemums. In the spring Hankuro had often seen children playing there and townspeople gathering herbs.

Halfway up the slope he came to the strip of land. As he had guessed, there was a path leading off in the direction of the samurai homes. Walking amid the tall weeds, Hankuro's baggy trousers soon became wet with dew. After a while the path disappeared, but he continued until he came to the samurai houses on the other side of the vacant lot. He clambered up a low retaining wall and found himself in a narrow passage between two large houses. He had waited until after ten o'clock before leaving home, so there was no sign of anybody still awake in the houses. Not a sound was to be heard.

Hankuro groped his way carefully along the alley until he came out onto a wider street. As he had hoped, he was almost directly opposite the rear gate of Honda's estate.

I'll have to climb that, he thought ruefully. It was lower than the main gate, though, and if he could find a foothold it should not be too difficult. From the end of the passage, he peered up and down the street, but there was no one in sight.

They're bound to be here somewhere, he thought.

He folded his arms and waited. From what Oriye had told him, he knew that the enemy's objective was to intercept the daimyo's letter at any cost. They knew that it had not yet been delivered, so they would be on the alert.

As he took another peek around the corner, he heard a sneeze on his right. A lookout was hiding in the shadows a few paces along the road. Two more sneezes followed in quick succession, but they sounded muffled, so the man had obviously covered his mouth and nose.

Hankuro took the opportunity to slip out of the passage and address the man.

"Sounds like you're coming down with a cold," he said sympathetically.

"Eh?"

The man had been sitting by the foot of the wall but sprang up, only to receive such a sharp blow to his solar plexus that he collapsed into Hankuro's arms with a moan. Hankuro lowered him to the ground and ran across the road to the gate. Jumping up, he managed to get one hand over the top of the gate and was scrabbling up when he heard several people rushing toward him. They must have realized something was amiss. Summoning every ounce of strength, Hankuro hauled himself up and succeeded in getting one elbow over the gate. Just as he thought he had reached the limits of his stamina, his foot found a rivet on the gate which he used for purchase to lever himself up. One of his pursuers jumped and struck out with his sword, but at that instant Hankuro swung himself over the gate and dropped inside. The sound of the sword hitting the gate echoed in the night. Hankuro remained crouching where he had landed and listened. Hearing nothing, he soon rose and walked through the wooded garden toward the darkened house.

Another thirty minutes passed before he found himself seated in one of the councilor's rooms. It had taken longer than expected for him to persuade the household guards that his intentions were honorable. Even then he had to wait for the councilor to appear. Honda was small and frail-looking, but he had a healthy complexion.

"They tell me that you're a messenger from Edo," Honda remarked, scrutinizing Hankuro with sharp eyes.

"No, I'm not," Hankuro replied hurriedly. "I just said that to gain admittance into your house. The real messenger is a young woman by the name of Oriye."

"Oriye?" Honda thought for a moment. "Ah yes, Shoji's daughter. That makes sense, but then who are you?"

"I am Shimada Hankuro of the construction corps."

"Shimada Hankuro? Are you Oriye's husband?"

"No, no," Hankuro replied, flustered. "I have a wife and family of my own."

"Yes, you are a bit old for Oriye. She must still be only fifteen or sixteen." His information was apparently out of date as she was clearly eighteen or nineteen years old. "That being the case, perhaps you can tell me why Shimada Hankuro, with a wife and family of his own, should decide to visit me at this hour."

Hankuro explained how he had managed to rescue Oriye the previous evening on his way home from Mishima. "She's recovering from her injuries in my house." He took out the letter. "So I am delivering the letter she brought from Edo."

Honda clapped his hands in sudden comprehension.

"Why didn't you say so earlier?" he demanded curtly, removing the wrapping and reading the letter by the lamp. "So His Lordship has made his decision," he murmured, looking visibly moved. Hankuro had no idea why the letter should evince such a reaction, but he was just glad his part in the affair was over.

"If that is all, I will take my leave now, sir," Hankuro said, starting to rise, but the councilor motioned for him to remain.

"Have you read this letter?"

"Yes." Hankuro anticipated a reprimand. It was a secret letter from the daimyo to his councilor, and whatever the circumstances he could expect to be censured for his presumption in reading it. "I apologize deeply for doing so."

"Did you understand the contents?"

"No, not at all." The text had seemed disjointed and to consist of a list of names.

"No, I don't suppose you would." The councilor wiggled his nose and suddenly looked like any friendly old man who wanted a chat. "The situation is like this . . ."

The daimyo, Samanokami Toshitsuna, was a sick man. He had

collapsed at his residence in Edo two years earlier and had been confined to his bed ever since. It was assumed that his eldest son, Rinnosuke, would be appointed his heir, but this had not been finalized, so Sugé Hannojo, the chief councilor in Edo, decided to discuss the matter with the daimyo to learn his views. However, whether the daimyo understood Sugé's anxieties or not, he gave no clear answer.

About six months before this, it had occurred to Honda that His Lordship might not want Rinnosuke to succeed him. There were two younger sons, Yogoro and Shinnosuke, born to the daimyo's mistress, who lived in a separate part of the castle. Honda wondered if the daimyo intended one of them to be his heir, but there was no way he could be certain of this.

Rinnosuke, the eldest son, excelled at both scholarship and the martial arts. He had his father's tempestuous nature and all the makings of a gifted leader. His younger brothers were both mild-mannered youths of average intelligence and ability. Yogoro, who turned twenty this year, liked studying but was only an average student.

However, despite his many merits, Rinnosuke was not without his faults. He was an avid hunter and loved hawking, but if the day did not go well he had a tendency to vent his frustration on his followers, with the result that they were reluctant to accompany him on his hunts. Although Honda did not know the details, it was rumored that one of Rinnosuke's men had been killed when he tried to escape from the domain after having been severely punished for a mistake during a hunt. In another incident, a farmer had crossed in front of Rinnosuke's horse and had been cut down for his lack of respect.

Yet another scandal involving Rinnosuke concerned the Sakubei irrigation channel he had built in the northern part of the domain despite a heated debate with the daimyo. The project had been suggested by Sakubei, the bailiff of the area, but the daimyo decreed that it was not worth the expense. Rinnosuke disagreed with his father. He had just turned twenty-one years of age and was beginning to show an interest in running the domain. In this case he had the support of the chief councilor, Misaka, who persuaded the daimyo to give his reluctant approval. However, the construction work through the mountains did not proceed smoothly, with the result that two hundred and seventy workers suffered sickness or injury, and fifty-six of them died.

Once the work was completed, however, water from the river that flowed through the northern part of the domain was diverted into areas of wilderness, creating three hundred and fifty acres of new paddies. As a result, Rinnosuke received high praise for his leadership abilities, but Honda wondered if the daimyo did not consider the lives of fifty-six farmers more important than the income from the extra three hundred and fifty acres under the plow.

It proved harder than Honda had thought to approach the daimyo and learn of his true intentions as regards his successor, for Chief Councilor Misaka had blocked all access to him.

Misaka had used his cooperation with Rinnosuke on the irrigation project as a means of deepening his relationship with the young man, regularly inviting him to his house and eventually succeeding in having him marry his third daughter. Thus, Misaka could not countenance the idea of anyone else assuming control of the domain, and he placed agents both in the domain and in Edo to thwart those who thought differently.

It was this obsessive behavior of Misaka's that provoked Honda to action. Of course, he was not against Rinnosuke taking over the reins of power. If that was the daimyo's wish, he would make every effort to ensure it was carried out, but if it was not, he would use every means at his disposal to prevent it. He did not like the way Misaka refused all discussion of the subject, which to him smacked of conspiracy.

His first task was to discover the daimyo's real intent, and to this effect he recruited several people he trusted who were about to travel to Edo for service there. Among them was Oriye's father, Shoji Shinzaemon.

In Edo, Misaka got wind of what Honda was doing, but he had no way of knowing which of the new arrivals were Honda's agents.

"This was the letter that Oriye was trying to deliver." Honda held it out to Hankuro and pointed to the writing. "Now you know enough to make sense of it. Here it says 'Yogoro,' which means that he wants Yogoro to succeed him, and then it says I should discuss this with Misaka, and if he does not agree he must be killed."

Hankuro remained silent.

"This is His Lordship's true wish. He has chosen mediocrity over ability. Don't you find that interesting, Tajima?"

The councilor sounded excited, though Hankuro could not understand why.

"My name is Shimada Hankuro."

"Oh, sorry. I think His Lordship feels that Rinnosuke's

temperament is a potential threat to the domain. He has decided that mediocrity is better suited to the peaceful world we live in. Now that we know his real feelings, we have to discuss the matter with Misaka. But this poses a problem."

"It is very late, sir, so if you will excuse me," said Hankuro bowing and making as if to leave. It was interesting to learn of the inner workings of clan politics, but it was all above his head and did not concern him. The identity of the next daimyo may be of crucial importance to Honda and Misaka, but it made little difference to a lowly member of the construction corps. His family had held the same post since his grandfather's time, and he thought this unlikely to change anytime soon, so there was little point in continuing the conversation.

"Wait, Tajima."

"It's Shimada, sir."

"I'm sorry. Wait, let's have some tea."

Honda clapped his hands to summon a servant, and almost immediately the door behind Hankuro slid open and a middle-aged samurai entered the room. Hankuro was surprised, but then remembered that Honda was not just a garrulous old gentleman but one of the most powerful members of the council. Naturally he had guards posted outside the room, ready to act if Hankuro proved to have any treacherous motives in mind.

Honda ordered tea to be brought.

"You said Oriye was attacked and you rescued her. I assume that means you're good with a sword?" Honda asked, becoming more affable.

"I'm a teacher at the Torii dojo," Hankuro replied with some pride. It was not often that a senior official inquired about his martial arts ability, and sword fighting was his one outstanding talent.

"Is that so, is that so?" Honda's eyes narrowed, and he looked at Hankuro contemplatively.

"Are you willing to help me?" he asked suddenly.

"Help in what way?"

"I have never believed in forming factions, so I have nobody to assist me. That is where Misaka and I differ. He has the backing of the district steward, Kumagai, as well Sugé Hannojo, the chief councilor in Edo, and Chamberlain Ozeki."

"Whose side is Vice Councilor Nakao Kuranosuke on?"

"He is too sick to carry out his duties at the castle, so he does not concern us. Anyway, he is weak-willed at the best of times." The councilor was not one to mince words. "The problem is that at some point I will have to confront Misaka, who has many followers while I have none."

"What about your retainers?"

"They are all useless when it comes to sword fighting," Honda replied, breaking into a wide, toothless smile.

That is hardly anything to smile about, Hankuro thought. Misaka had known that whatever the contents of the letter, it could not be allowed to fall into Honda's hands. Now that it had, there was every possibility that Misaka would decide to have Honda killed. Not only did Misaka have the power to do this, but he was also obsessed with the idea of Rinnosuke becoming the next daimyo. That was why Oriye had said it was so urgent that Honda receive the letter without the Misaka faction knowing. Now he realized how unfortunate it was that he had been seen entering the estate.

"What do you intend to do?" Hankuro asked.

"First, I have to arrange a meeting with Misaka inside the castle. I will confront him with His Lordship's letter and demand that he abandon all plans of Rinnosuke succeeding his father. I doubt he will agree, however, in which case we will have to settle the matter with swords. I have little confidence in my abilities in that area, although I used to be something of a swordsman in my youth."

"So when you ask for my help, you want me to kill him."

"I am not asking you to strike the first blow. I will do that. I just want you to help if it looks as though I am losing."

Hankuro remained silent.

"Do you refuse? I am afraid I cannot permit that. As a retainer of the clan, you have no choice in the matter. I have explained the whole situation to you, so you can see that I am in the right."

There was a clear threat in Honda's tone, and Hankuro regretted having boasted of his skill with the sword, but it was too late now.

"What will happen then?"

"Oh, that's simple," Honda replied with another smile. "I will assemble all the retainers, read them the letter, and then address them."

"What do you want to talk about?" Jinnai asked as they settled into one of the rooms at the Imoriya.

"Let's have a drink first."

They had arrived early and were the only customers in the tavern. A waitress brought their saké and was about to light the lamp in the room when Hankuro stopped her. Enough light came from the doorway for them to see, and if the room was dark they would notice other customers arriving. Outside, the town was still bathed in June sunshine.

"Very soon your lieutenant will order you to request some leave. I want you to do as he says without asking any questions."

"Take leave?" Jinnai looked at him curiously. "I can't do that. You know things are not going well with my wife. Goodness knows what she'd say if I sat at home all day."

"There's a good reason for it," Hankuro replied, lowering his voice. "When you're on leave, you won't have time to lounge about the house. We've been assigned to guard Councilor Honda."

"What's all this about? I don't understand."

Hankuro explained the situation while Jinnai listened in silence, except for an occasional groan. However, this did not prevent him from drinking steadily, and his right hand never seemed still. Hankuro, on the other hand, was so busy talking that he had not been able to take a single sip, and he was beginning to feel exasperated.

"Then what happened?"

"Wait. Let me drink, too." He hastily downed two or three cupfuls of saké before continuing.

"The councilor is so involved with the political situation that he has no time to think of his own protection. Misaka's men will be trying to get the letter from Honda, but if they fail they'll have no choice but to kill him."

"That's true."

"They're not going to attack him at home. It would attract too much attention. Instead they'll get him in the castle or on his way there or back. So he can't take any chances."

"I see."

"Hey, stop! That's my fish you're eating," Hankuro protested. "Anyway, Honda's realized the danger he's in and has asked me to help. Knowing the situation, I couldn't very well refuse."

"Rather you than me!"

"You don't understand. You see, I mentioned your name as well."

"You did what?" With a brusque movement, Jinnai put down his saké cup and chopsticks. "You're saying you want me to help the councilor?"

"Yes. We've been friends a long time, so I'm hoping you'll agree."

"Hmm." Jinnai folded his arms. "By help, I suppose you mean you want me to be a guard."

"Not exactly."

"What do you mean by that?"

"That's what I thought at first, but the councilor has no one to help him. Misaka has built up his faction in the clan and can call upon twenty or thirty men at a moment's notice. Honda has nobody, but he still means to go against them alone if he has to. Don't you think that shows courage?"

"I suppose so," Jinnai said grudgingly.

"Anyway, he's asked us to help. It's the first time he has turned to anyone, so I couldn't refuse, could I?"

"Yes, I see that. But we're still outnumbered. What about Tomono Zensuke? Can't you get him to join us?"

"Tomono . . ." Hankuro's expression clouded as he recalled the events of the previous evening.

It had been past midnight when Hankuro finally left Honda's estate. Honda's retainers had accompanied him as far as the gate, but as Hankuro did not think anyone would be watching the house at that hour, he set off alone. However, he had only taken a few steps when four or five men sprang out of the dark and attacked. Misaka must have decided to deprive Honda of any supporters he might enlist and isolate him in his estate.

The attackers were masked, so Hankuro could not recognize any of them, but they were all accomplished fighters who put him on the defensive. Among them was a short man whose powerful thrusts he was hard-pressed to parry. He was only able to get away when he cut his opponent's wrist, making him break off the attack. He himself was not unscathed, for he had a gash on his arm.

"Look at this." Hankuro pulled up his sleeve and removed the white bandage around his arm.

"Hmm, looks like a thrust wound," Jinnai remarked with a frown. "But that does not mean it was Tomono."

"True, but this man was short, and there aren't many who fight like him."

"I don't like the sound of this."

Hankuro clapped his hands to summon a waitress and order more saké. He noticed that some lamps had been lit and three merchants were drinking at the long table. When the girl arrived with the saké, she asked if she should light their lamp, but Hankuro said no. There was sufficient light for the moment.

"So are you in or not?"

"I'm not sure."

"It'll be a good chance to show your wife what you're capable of."

"You think so?"

"Yes. Since I became involved in all this, my wife's whole attitude has changed. You should have seen her when she was treating my cut."

"Hmm."

"It's your chance to prove yourself, Jinnai."

"I suppose I don't have a choice. All right, I'll help," he said finally, looking quite sober. Hankuro guessed it would take a lot to make him weep in his cups that night. Seeing this, Hankuro thought he would add an extra sweetener.

"Who knows, it may even result in promotion."

On a hot summer's day about a month later, Honda confronted Misaka to settle the matter.

The councilor was in the castle's Peony Room, seated behind a table, while Hankuro and Jinnai were hiding in the adjoining room. The doors and windows of the Peony Room were wide open, letting in a cool breeze, but the room where Hankuro and Jinnai were concealed had no windows and it felt like being in a steam bath. Hankuro could feel the perspiration trickling down his body, and, turning around, he saw Jinnai wiping his brow with his forearm. All was quiet in the castle as the seconds ticked by.

Suddenly they heard voices and footsteps hurrying in their direction.

"Are you trying to make a fool of me, Honda?" an angry voice demanded. "I was told you would be in the Chrysanthemum Room, so I went there only to learn that you were waiting for me here. What do you mean by summoning me like this? Do you have something to discuss?"

"Please calm yourself and take a seat," Honda said quietly. "Of course I want to talk. That is why I asked you to come."

Although Misaka was the senior of the two, Honda was a blood relation of the daimyo, so his family status was higher. This was reflected in the dignified tone of his voice.

Both men then lowered their voices so nothing further could be heard. Hankuro looked at Jinnai, who had turned quite pale with fear and was licking his lips. Time passed slowly.

Suddenly Misaka's deep voice boomed out. "I will never agree to that."

"But it is what His Lordship wishes."

"It's a conspiracy."

"Think what you like, but you cannot deny what is written."

"I don't believe it! The letter is a fake!"

"Be prudent, Misaka."

Some curses were shouted, followed by the sound of something falling.

"It is His Lordship's will!" shouted Honda.

Hankuro and Jinnai exchanged glances before flinging open the doors and entering the room. Misaka and Honda were standing face to face with their swords drawn, and two samurai guards who had accompanied Misaka had rushed in from the corridor.

The next moment total confusion erupted. Hankuro made

straight for Misaka while Jinnai took on the two samurai. Misaka stopped fighting Honda and turned to Hankuro. He was a large man with a powerful build, and his sword whistled as he swung it, but Hankuro dodged and, slipping inside Misaka's guard, drew his short sword and thrust it into the man's chest.

"It is His Lordship's will," he muttered.

Misaka's eyes bulged in disbelief, then he fell to the floor with a thud before Hankuro had a chance to catch him.

Jinnai hurried to his friend's side.

"One of them got away," he said, blood dripping from his sword.

"That went well," Honda said, sheathing his sword. The shoulder of his kimono had been cut in two, and one half was hanging down his chest.

"Chief Censor Terauchi Hachirobei is waiting in the Bell Room. Please fetch him. You have nothing to fear as we have already come to an agreement. He is particularly partial to salted salmon, so I invited him to my house the other evening and after a few drinks I gave him half a fish. Now he is on our side."

Half a fish did not sound like much of a bribe, and Hankuro glanced at Jinnai in surprise, but Honda appeared very confident.

It was just as Honda had said. The censor had been bought for half a salted salmon. He hurried to the Peony Room and quickly gave orders for the mess to be cleaned up. While that was being done, Honda summoned Vice Councilor Nakao Kuranosuke from home where he lay in his sickbed, and after some secret discussion they called Misaka's accomplices—District Steward Kumagai, Lieutenant Matsuzaka, and Shindo Jidayu—and reprimanded them for their part in the plot. With Misaka out of the way, Honda was the sole figure of authority, and when they were shown the daimyo's letter, they had no alternative but to submit.

However, their retainers were not so easily discouraged. By the time Honda had finished attending to all the details, it was past seven o'clock, and he set off for home with three retainers in addition to Hankuro and Jinnai. As the party walked beside the castle's outer moat, a group of ten samurai suddenly sprang out from beneath the embankment surrounding the horse paddock.

"You take Tomono," Hankuro said quickly to Jinnai, as he spotted their former friend among the group, his face distorted with rage.

In the fierce encounter that followed, Honda and his retainers had to draw their swords to defend themselves. Jinnai managed to lure Tomono to one side while Hankuro placed himself in front of the councilor and bore the brunt of the attack. He was forced to wound two of the more accomplished swordsmen, but the others he merely rendered unconscious with the back of his blade.

Seeing the hopelessness of the situation, the last three attackers ran off. Hankuro turned just in time to see Jinnai deflect an upward thrust from Tomono and respond with a blow to his side. Tomono jumped back and put his hand to his wound before falling awkwardly to the ground.

Hankuro walked over to Jinnai.

"If only he'd run off with the others, I'd have let him go," Jinnai said with a troubled expression.

The sun had set, and as the flaming hues faded from the clouds, the air took on an evening chill. The deepening darkness soon enveloped the body of their erstwhile friend, now lying motionless at their feet.

Autumn had arrived in the northern domain, and although the sun was shining as Hankuro and Jinnai headed home for the day, there was no warmth in it.

"Strange that we haven't heard anything, isn't it?" commented Jinnai.

"It is," Hankuro replied dejectedly. He had the same thought as his friend. They had played a major role in the disturbances surrounding the selection of the new daimyo, yet neither had received any reward.

The old daimyo had died during the August heat and had been succeeded by his second son, Yogoro, so Councilor Honda's strategy had been successful, but only just in time. Before the daimyo's death, Honda had summoned the chief councilor in Edo, and after discussions with him and Vice Councilor Nakao, it was decided that Rinnosuke should start a new branch family with an annual income of 40,000 bushels of rice. Misaka's death was blamed on illness, and he was succeeded by his eldest son, Hikojiro. The samurai in the clan had all been notified of the letter naming the daimyo's choice of successor, so Honda's decrees met with no opposition.

Hankuro and Jinnai anticipated some kind of promotion once the situation had settled down. The young daimyo had already traveled to Edo to meet the shogun and life had returned to normal, but still they heard nothing.

"The truth is I've had another row with my wife. She hasn't

said a word to me since last night," Jinnai said despondently. "It would be a godsend if we were to get a raise now."

"It would indeed," Hankuro replied. As it happened, his situation was similar. From the night he had carried Oriye home, his wife had become a different person. Obedient and attentive, she had looked after the injured woman conscientiously and had done whatever he asked. She always had a smile on her face, and had bragged so much about him to Oriye that the younger woman had seemed almost jealous.

However, after things calmed down and Oriye recovered sufficiently to return to her home in Byobu, Misa reverted to her old self, nagging, sulking, and refusing to speak to Hankuro. They were forever squabbling, and their daughter always took Misa's side.

Jinnai suddenly stopped in his tracks.

"You don't suppose that—no, that couldn't be our only reward," he said.

"Surely not!"

The two of them stood stock-still in the middle of the street and looked at each other.

Shortly after the events at the castle, a melon had been delivered to each of their houses. The melons had been sent by Honda and were carefully wrapped in straw, but there was only one for each household. The weather was hot at the time, and Hankuro had chilled his by placing it in the well for half a day. The melon had been delicious, but now he could hardly remember the taste. After all, it was some time ago.

"No, that can't be it," Hankuro said gloomily.

They resumed walking.

"Did you mention anything to your wife about a promotion?" Hankuro asked glumly.

"Yes, but I did say there was only a slight chance."

"Me, too."

They walked on in silence. When they came to the junction at Teppo where they usually parted, they both stopped, and with a nod to each other set off for the taverns of Mishima. Hankuro detected a desperate glint in Jinnai's eye, and he guessed that his friend would be crying in his cups tonight. With a resigned expression on his face, he followed Jinnai down the road.

Kozuru

Kanna Kichizaemon and his wife, Tomé, were renowned for their quarrels. In fact, their reputation had spread beyond their neighborhood to the whole town, and Kichizaemon's superior, Lieutenant Hyodo Yahei, had had to reprimand him sternly more than once since this kind of behavior reflected badly on samurai in general.

Whenever he was rebuked, Kichizaemon would become contrite and apologize profusely. "I'll make certain it never happens again," he would say, looking suitably repentant. However, his resolve never lasted very long, and within a few days the couple would be fighting again. They would yell at each other so loudly that passersby could not help but stop and listen.

Of course, this was not to say that no other samurai families had altercations of this sort, but they usually had enough self-control to ensure that their quarrels could not be heard beyond the walls of their homes. Kichizaemon and his wife, on the other hand, behaved less like samurai and more like the lower-class townsfolk living in row houses, whose voices would often echo up and down the streets.

Kichizaemon and his wife were the only occupants of their house, so it was evident who was responsible for the noise. They had an elderly maid, but she was a pale, nervous woman who would surely have fainted had Kichizaemon ever shouted at her in the same way.

"Talk to me like that and I'll make sure you never speak again!" Kichizaemon would bellow with such fury that anyone who did not know him might worry what his next action would be.

"Go ahead, then, and do it," Tomé replied, not sounding the least upset. Her voice was deeper than her husband's, but she had the same disregard for propriety and the neighbors could hear her every word. "What are you waiting for? If you think killing me will gratify your ancestors, then go ahead!"

"This fish is rotten!" Kichizaemon shouted, their argument suddenly taking a turn toward the mundane. "If you expect me to eat this, you're not fit to run the house."

Realizing that it was just a trivial row about the evening meal, those who had stopped to listen soon lost interest. Neighbors would frown and close their shutters for the night. The quarrel was obviously a lot of fuss about nothing.

Kichizaemon's temper was legendary. In his younger days he was said to have chased his wife around the garden with his sword raised. Now that he was over fifty and Tomé was nearing that age, their conflicts were limited to shouting matches in which, most people agreed, he was usually the loser.

Yet it would be wrong to assume that the couple was always at loggerheads. Far from it. On days that Kichizaemon was off duty, the two could be seen working side by side in the garden or visiting the local temple together, oblivious to the notoriety their fights had achieved.

Actually, the problem stemmed from the fact that when Kichizaemon and Tomé married, he had been adopted into Tomé's family, meaning that he had taken on her father's surname, rank, and income. Even the house they were living in was hers, a fact she habitually reminded him of. The neighbors were accustomed to their arguments by this time, and they knew that Kichizaemon's bark was worse than his bite. Although they feigned disapproval, secretly they enjoyed listening to each drama as it unfolded. The only aspect that gave them cause for concern was that the couple was on the threshold of old age but they still had no heir.

Tomé had not been blessed with children, and when she passed child-bearing age, she and Kichizaemon had started looking for a son to adopt to ensure the continuation of the family name. However, they had never found anyone they considered suitable.

"The way they carry on, who'd want to be adopted by them?" the neighbors would comment. Discussions of their prospects of adopting someone would invariably end on this note, and by now everyone was resigned to the situation.

Kichizaemon worked in the construction corps and was paid an annual stipend of 500 bushels of rice. Although his household could by no means be described as rich, it was just right in terms of size and income for a man seeking to be adopted. Unlike larger and richer families, there were fewer rules and traditions to be observed in daily life, yet at the same time the family was far from poor. Moreover, the couple had no relatives living with them for an adopted son to have to worry about.

Positions within a clan were generally handed down from father to eldest son, and there was otherwise very little chance of promotion. As a result, many second and third sons of samurai families had no prospects of work and spent their lives living off parents and siblings. They liked to say that they were prepared to marry into any family as long as the bride was a woman and there was sufficient income to ensure three square meals a day. However, Kichizaemon had approached several such young men through intermediaries, but his offer had consistently been rejected.

Everybody agreed that the sole reason for this lay in the feuding between Kichizaemon and Tomé, which scared off even the boldest young men. Nobody said as much to Kichizaemon's face, but they were all convinced of it in their hearts. The inability to find anyone to adopt became a source of further friction between the couple, with Tomé criticizing Kichizaemon for being incapable of finding an heir and Kichizaemon blaming Tomé for not producing children. The battles continued, providing endless entertainment for the neighbors. It was ironic, however, that it was precisely these fights over an heir that made young men even more reluctant to come forward.

One day Kichizaemon came in through the garden gate with a young girl in tow. Tomé was busy removing insects from her chrysanthemum plants. Chrysanthemums produce beautiful flowers, but are easily destroyed by insects eating the leaves.

"Hello, who's this?" Tomé asked, straightening up and looking at the girl, who was half-hidden behind Kichizaemon's back. She was young and was dressed in traveling clothes.

"Well, you see," said Kichizaemon, looking at the girl uncertainly, "it's a long story . . ."

"I'm sure it is. Go ahead, I'm listening."

"We can't talk out here. Let's go inside."

Kichizaemon had no wish to be overheard and entered the house without waiting for Tomé. The girl stood where she was, her eyes fixed on the ground. She was wearing a traveler's straw sandals and leggings as well as gloves, and in one hand she was holding a large straw hat. It was obvious from her clothes and hairstyle that she was from the samurai class, but Tomé was rather taken aback that the girl made no move to greet her.

"You'd better come in too," she said.

The girl looked up and Tomé saw that she was quite beautiful, with large eyes and a small, shapely mouth. Probably as a result of fatigue from her travels, her face was pale and she had a blank expression. She appeared to be about seventeen or eighteen years of age.

At Tomé's urging, the girl walked toward the house, moving as though in a daze. Tomé thought she looked exhausted.

"Where have you come from?" she asked as they entered the house, but the girl remained silent and her expression did not change.

How strange, thought Tomé.

"She's tired. Let her sleep a bit first," Kichizaemon said once they were all inside. Something about the girl was clearly troubling him, for he was waiting uncertainly in the room without even going to change his clothes.

Tomé led the girl to the guest room at the rear of the house and laid out a bed for her. She returned to find Kichizaemon still hovering near the entrance hall. She made him change his clothes, then prepared some green tea and asked him once more about the girl. It was beginning to get dark, but it was still too early to prepare the evening meal.

"I hope you're not going to tell me that she's your child."

"Don't be stupid!" Kichizaemon replied, momentarily flustered.

He had a broad, square-jawed face, with bushy eyebrows over large, sunken eyes. Tomé did not believe he was the type of man who would have had a child with a mistress, and she had only asked to make doubly sure. His look of confusion afforded her some amusement.

"I found her on Komai Bridge."

"Found her?"

"Yes. I went to check on the embankments there on my way home . . ."

The Goken River ran through the center of the castle town. At one spot a mile above Komai Bridge and at two other places downriver the stone embankments had been washed away during the summer floods. A month had passed since the construction corps had handled the repairs, so Kichizaemon's superior had sent him to check the retaining walls.

When Kichizaemon reached the bridge, he saw the girl leaning over the railing watching the water rushing past below. Kichizaemon assumed she was just another traveler taking a rest and thought no more about it. He climbed down the riverbank and walked upstream, wading into the river where it was shallow to make sure the wall was holding. He then went downriver to inspect the repairs, and as he passed beneath the bridge he noticed that the girl was still standing there. However, he paid her no further attention.

It was some distance from the bridge to the other two places that needed to be checked, and when he reached them he lay down on his stomach on the riverbank to get as close as he could to the wall. As before, he then waded into the shallows and crossed to the other bank to check the wall and to see how the water was flowing past the repairs. Everything appeared to be in order.

Kichizaemon was a conscientious worker. He performed the necessary inspections painstakingly and naturally forgot all about the girl on the bridge. Once he had finished, he climbed back up the bank, and it was while he was stretching to relax his muscles that he noticed the girl still standing on the bridge. The sun was already beginning to set, lending a soft golden tint to the yellow of the ripening rice in the fields. The girl was enveloped in the same golden glow.

I wonder what she's doing, he thought. She had been there too long for someone taking a rest. For the first time he began to take an interest in her and decided to speak to her.

"When I got back to the bridge," he recounted to Tomé, "I asked her what she was doing, but she didn't reply."

Upon hearing him speak, the girl had turned and looked at him vacantly. Her face was beautiful, but devoid of expression.

"I asked her several questions, but she just looked at me in silence. I didn't know what to do, but if I just left her there, goodness knows what might happen to her when it got dark. That's why I brought her back with me."

"You did the right thing. You couldn't have done anything else under the circumstances."

"As far as I can tell, she's not mad. But she's been driven into a kind of stupor. Something must have happened to her. She'll probably recover after a good night's sleep, and we can ask her about herself then."

"Yes, that's best."

"Did she say anything to you?"

"Not a word."

"I wonder if she'll talk tomorrow. If there's no change, I'll have to report her to the magistrate's office."

Tomé made no reply.

"It could be a problem, though," he said, his head lowered in thought. Then he looked up suddenly in agitation. "I wonder if she's really gone to bed. You don't suppose she might have slipped out, do you?"

"Don't be silly."

"Go and take a look, will you? Just a peep."

At Kichizaemon's urging, Tomé left the room and crept down the corridor to the girl's rom, but she soon returned.

"She's in bed and fast asleep."

The couple looked at each other and faint smiles appeared on both their faces. It had always been just the two of them in the house, and the thought of someone else sleeping in the other room filled them with a certain excitement.

When Kichizaemon returned home late the next day, he found the girl on the veranda. She was sitting decorously on a cushion Tomé had placed there, her back ramrod straight, looking up at the moon. It was a beautifully clear night. The moon was almost full, and Kichizaemon had been admiring it on his way home. What was strange, though, was that although this was his house, the girl made no effort to greet him as he walked to the house from the gate.

After changing his clothes, he sat down to dinner. "Has she eaten?" he asked Tomé in a low voice, with a nod in the girl's direction.

"Yes, she has. And she said it was good."

"At least she can talk then," he said, then paused. "Did she say anything else?"

"Yes," Tomé replied enthusiastically. "I asked her several questions, and she answered most of them."

"And"—Kichizaemon paused while he bit off a piece of dried fish—"what did you learn about her?"

"Nothing. She doesn't remember anything. She doesn't know where she's from, where she was going, or even the names of her parents or relatives. What can it mean?"

Kichizaemon popped a crispy radish pickle into his mouth and chewed noisily. Normally, Tomé would complain if he did this or if he talked with his mouth full, asking him sarcastically if that was the way lower-ranking samurai were brought up. The couple had been together for thirty years, but Tomé never missed an opportunity to point out that she came from a better family. This would lead to an immediate quarrel, but not today. She sat quietly as she waited for him to finish, although he could tell from her eyes that she was growing impatient. He swallowed the mouthful at last.

"That's a problem."

"The only thing she remembers is her name. Can you guess what it is?"

"How can I?"

"Kozuru."

"Hmm, Kozuru." It meant "little crane." He glanced over at the girl, then back to Tomé. Their eyes met and they both smiled. "What a beautiful name!"

Kichizaemon finished his meal, and as he sat drinking his tea he repeated her name. It suited their strange young guest.

"Has she been watching the moon all evening?" he asked.

"Yes. I think she's trying to remember something about herself, poor soul," Tomé replied softly.

"She reminds me of the princess in that fairy tale. You know, the one who was found as a baby inside a bamboo grove and grew into a beautiful woman in a matter of months. They said she would sit gazing sadly up at the night sky, waiting for the people from the moon to come and take her back home."

"Yes, she is like that! Anyway, have you decided what you're going to do?"

"About what?"

"About reporting her to the magistrate's office."

He knew it was his duty to do so. He had been hoping the girl would remember something about herself, but three days had passed and he still could not bring himself to act.

"I suppose I should."

"Why don't we wait a little longer and see what happens?"

"Hmm."

"She's not well. She can't even remember her parents' names, so even if you do take her to the magistrate's office, they won't learn any more about her."

"That's true."

"They'll ask her a lot of questions. And it would be such a pity if they just locked her up afterwards."

"I'm sure they won't do that."

"Don't be so sure," Tomé said, showing her irritation. "You're the one who found her, so why can't you be a bit more sympathetic?"

"I am being sympathetic," Kichizaemon replied, looking cross. "All I'm saying is that it's our duty to report her."

"But if you do, there's no telling how the magistrate will treat her. After all, it's his job to suspect the worst of people."

"That's the way women think. You have to understand that there are certain formalities that have to be followed before you're allowed to let anyone live in your house. That's all I am saying, so stop whining."

"What do you mean by 'whining'? You can't talk to me like that!"

"Be quiet!"

As usual, the argument was growing more heated and their voices began to rise. Just then a strange sound made them both fall silent. They looked toward the veranda—Kozuru had left her seat on the cushion and was sitting bolt upright on the bare wooden floor. She was looking at them, and tears were streaming down her cheeks. It was the sound of her sobbing that had made them stop arguing.

"What's wrong, Kozuru?" Tomé asked, hurrying to her side and putting her arm around her shoulder.

"Please don't quarrel! Please don't do that anymore!" Kozuru pleaded, tears still running down her face.

"Now look what you've done, shouting like that!" Tomé said, glaring at Kichizaemon. Her voice then became so gentle that it was hard to believe it came from the same person. "Don't worry. We're not quarreling. I was just scolding my obstinate husband. How do you feel? You're still not well. Why don't you go back to bed?"

Tomé led Kozuru to her room while Kichizaemon stepped out onto the veranda and looked up dejectedly at the moon. He could not understand why a girl of her age should cry like that. He felt baffled as well as frustrated.

Kichizaemon reported Kozuru's presence to his superior, Lieutenant Hyodo, and to the magistrate's office. In fact, even before he visited the latter, the lieutenant had already submitted the request for him and Kichizaemon was allowed to remain in charge of the girl. She had been asked two or three cursory questions, but when it became apparent that she had lost her memory, just as Kichizaemon had claimed, the officials were only too glad that someone was willing to take her off their hands.

Hyodo took a more sarcastic attitude.

"So you want to look after her, do you? I don't know anything about her, but I bet she won't be able to stand living in your house for more than three days."

He was of course referring to Kichizaemon and Tomé's reputation for quarreling. Kichizaemon felt like telling him how wrong he was, for the girl had already been with them for five days. However, he did not want to antagonize the lieutenant for fear of being told he could not look after the girl any longer.

Since Kichizaemon had been granted official permission to care for the girl, Kozuru was now free to leave the house and go into town. Tomé was overjoyed. She took her to the temple to pray, to visit the garden of a rich merchant who opened it to the public once a year to show off his chrysanthemums, and to the stores.

"Today we're going to buy you a new kimono," Tomé announced one morning. She took Kozuru to a store that sold cotton and linen but specialized in silk. One of the assistants who dealt with samurai families recognized Tomé as a long-time customer and hurried over as they entered.

"Show me something that will suit this girl. We want one formal kimono and another for everyday wear," Tomé demanded.

"Certainly." The assistant went to the cupboards at the rear of the shop and soon returned with his arms loaded with bolts of material. "She's such a beauty. Excuse me if I'm being forward, but I thought you had no children. Who is she?"

"A distant relative. She will be staying with us for a while."

Kozuru stood and watched passively as the assistant held up various fabrics against her to see how she would look in each. Tomé was enjoying herself immensely: shopping for a young, attractive girl was a pleasure she had never experienced before.

Life would have been so different if I'd had a daughter, she thought. She had spent the twenty years since her parents died living with a husband she did not even particularly like. It seemed a shadow of an existence.

Kichizaemon and Tomé lived in Fukiya, the samurai quarter, where women were seldom seen on the street, unlike in the town's bustling merchant quarter. For this reason, Tomé's recent strolls with the mysterious girl soon became the subject of much gossip. Frequently, the two found themselves meeting neighbors who just happened to be coming out of their gates as they passed, seemingly on some errand or other. Needless to say, their real motive was to see the girl with their own eyes.

"What a pretty young lady," they would exclaim, as they caught a glimpse of Kozuru hiding behind Tomé. "A relative of yours, is she?"

"Yes, a distant relative. She'll be staying with us for a while," Tomé would reply with some pride. She was finally making up for all the years she had been childless, and she walked with her head held high.

As Kozuru's health improved, her complexion regained its bloom. Tomé would occasionally ask if she remembered anything about her past, but Kozuru would simply look sad and shake her head.

Time passed, and she settled into her new home. On days when the maid was off, Kozuru would do all the cooking, a task at which she excelled. She also cleaned the house until it was spotless, and her flower arrangements were done in accordance with the rules of that art. Sometimes she would offer to massage Tomé's shoulders, which delighted the old woman no end.

From Kozuru's accomplishments, Tomé deduced that the girl could not have been brought up in a very rich or powerful samurai family, or she would not have been able to cook. Yet her family was obviously respectable because her manners were impeccable. She felt keenly for the girl's parents, who must be worried to distraction, but until Kozuru remembered something of her former life there was nothing to be done.

Although Kozuru could not recall her past, as her complexion improved so her conversation became more animated. Occasionally, she would even laugh, which made her look more beautiful than ever.

One evening Kichizaemon was sitting beside Tomé, who was sewing a kimono for Kozuru.

"She's looking much better now. Has she remembered anything?" he asked his wife.

"No. Whenever I ask, she looks so sad that recently I've made it a rule to avoid the subject."

"It can't be helped. We can only wait and hope her memory comes back naturally."

"Do you think it will?"

"I've no idea."

"You know, I'm sure she must be an eldest child."

"What makes you say that?"

"I'm just sure of it," Tomé said firmly. "She's very thoughtful and well brought up."

"You think so?"

"Yes. For instance, while I was sewing today she came and massaged my shoulders, saying they must be stiff. She knew where all the pressure points were and has obviously had a lot of practice."

"She never offers to massage me," Kichizaemon responded moodily.

Tomé laughed gaily and thought how much their life had changed since Kozuru had arrived. The couple never tired of talking about her.

"No need to be jealous. She thinks of you, too."

"I'm not jealous."

"You enjoyed the fish and pickled vegetables tonight, didn't you?"

"Yes, it's one of my favorites."

"I know. When I mentioned it to Kozuru, she wanted to make it specially for you."

"So that explains why the meals have improved lately." He said it gruffly, but there was a twinkle in his eye.

Tomé stole a look at him, then resumed her sewing.

"What will happen to her if she never regains her memory?" she asked.

"She must have parents somewhere, and it would break their hearts if she never returned. I'm sure she'll remember something soon."

"But what if she doesn't?"

"If we knew for certain that she's not going to regain her memory . . ." He folded his arms and closed his eyes. "If that happens we'll have to adopt her. There's no other way," he said, lowering his voice.

"Yes, you're right." Tomé replied, unable to conceal her delight. Guiltily the two looked toward the corridor to make sure no one had overheard them.

"Make yourself at home," Katsuma Jusuke said warmly as Kichizaemon entered the private room in the restaurant. Although Katsuma was four or five years younger, his rank as assistant lieutenant of the construction corps made him Kichizaemon's immediate superior. "How about a drink?"

When the saké arrived, Katsuma politely filled Kichizaemon's cup. "Do you know the reason I invited you today?"

Kichizaemon made no reply.

"You once asked me about adopting the second son of Hashimoto Hikosuke. I wonder if you've decided on a suitable heir yet."

Oh, not again, Kichizaemon thought. It was the fifth time he had been approached in this way. He struggled to stifle a scornful laugh. Six months had passed since Kozuru had joined his household, and Kichizaemon and Tomé now regarded her as their daughter. If Kozuru should regain her memory, or if her parents found her, the couple had decided to ask their permission to adopt her formally, and they might agree if she was not an only child.

In these past six months, rumors of a young beauty living in

Kichizaemon's house had spread throughout the domain. The general belief was that she had been adopted by the childless couple, and all at once any number of young men appeared eager to join the household.

This sudden interest manifested itself in a variety of ways. Neighborhood women who had never been particularly friendly would drop by on the flimsiest excuse to subject Kozuru to scrutiny. Or acne-ridden young men would greet Kichizaemon as he passed the sword fighting dojo on his way to the castle, which had never happened before. They seemed to be indicating their willingness to be adopted, but Kichizaemon felt nothing but disgust for them and walked on without giving them a glance. There was no need to rush into things. Kozuru was so attractive that once they adopted her there would be no shortage of suitors.

One young man had even come to Kichizaemon requesting to be taught the flute. Kichizaemon had studied sword fighting since his youth but had never excelled at it. However, at the same time he had also taken up the flute and in this he had made remarkable progress. His teacher had even gone so far as to say that if he persevered he might well gain a reputation as a flautist.

A little after his twentieth birthday, however, Kichizaemon had been adopted by Tomé's family and had given up serious practice of the instrument. He did not regret this, for although he enjoyed music it had never been more than a hobby to him. Up until ten years ago, elegant strains of flute music could often be heard emanating from his house, in between the quarrels.

Kichizaemon had no idea how the young man knew about his flute playing. He had merely asked Kichizaemon to teach him, saying how much he liked the instrument, but Kichizaemon refused out of hand. It was obvious the youth just wanted an excuse to visit so he could talk to Kozuru. If he was truly interested in the flute, why had he not asked for lessons six months earlier, before Kozuru arrived?

Moreover, four people had approached him with requests for formal adoption. In fact, if Katsuma's was included, that would make it five. Kichizaemon had no interest in Katsuma's offer, though. The previous year he had sought Katsuma's help in adopting Hashimoto's second son but had been refused. The elder Hashimoto was a relative of Katsuma's, but the family's annual stipend was only 375 bushels of rice, so it was not as if Kichizaemon were asking for the son of a wealthy family. Despite this, his offer had been rejected point-blank. Kichizaemon remembered that this had led to another big quarrel with Tomé.

It now transpired that the young man was still unmarried and living at home, but, even so, Kichizaemon could not bring himself to show any enthusiasm for Katsuma's offer.

"Nothing has been settled yet. We've been approached by several people and we need time to reach a decision."

"Oh," Katsuma's eyes widened in surprise. "So I'm too late, am I?" he said, regret tingeing his voice.

"No, no. I haven't given anybody a definite answer. I need to discuss it with my wife and daughter to learn what they wish."

Thinking back to the time last year when he had prostrated himself before his superior, begging for help, it felt wonderful to be able to say this. That events could have taken such a turn was beyond his wildest expectations.

"In any case, please consider my offer," Katsuma said, with an unexpectedly deep bow. "The Hashimoto family has heard that you have a beautiful and good-natured young woman staying with you, and Sakunosuke is most eager to meet her."

Sakunosuke was the second son in question. His pleasing appearance and agreeable disposition had been why Kichizaemon had wanted to adopt him in the first place, but he had been refused. Now that Kozuru was living with them Sakunosuke had done a complete about-face, and Kichizaemon realized he was singularly lacking in sincerity.

"The girl's name is Kozuru, but for various reasons we have not yet decided whether to adopt her or not. She may return to her parents, in which case would Sakunosuke still be willing to be adopted by us?"

"I'm afraid I can't speak for the young man," Katsuma replied hastily. His reaction implied that, without Kozuru, the offer would be off. "I'd heard you'd already adopted the girl. Now you tell me that it isn't so."

"As I mentioned, we have reasons for not submitting a formal adoption request to the authorities yet."

"Well, get matters settled soon. Then I'll let you have Sakunosuke." Perhaps the drink had gone to Katsuma's head, for he was becoming increasingly peremptory. "You're getting on in years, and it's best to get this finalized without further delay."

"I agree. When I get home, I'll discuss it with them," Kichizaemon replied, savoring the situation to the fullest.

"Let's turn down Katsuma first," Kichizaemon said. "I don't like his pompous manner. After all, Hashimoto's income is not even as large as mine, so who does he think he is?"

"Are you sure that's the right thing to do? Katsuma is your superior, so won't it affect your position at the castle?"

"Don't worry. Katsuma doesn't have a good reputation in the construction corps. What's important is for us to choose the right person."

"I agree we must choose somebody suitable for Kozuru."

"We can eliminate Hashimoto Sakunosuke, then. Who's next? Fujii Shinroku. No, he's no use, either. He's a nephew of the district magistrate, but he's a third son and something of a troublemaker. Do you remember that incident in the Kamei pleasure quarter about two years ago, when he injured someone in a brawl?"

"Oh, I didn't know about that. He was suggested by Ohara's wife."

"It is good for a man to have lots of energy, but we don't want anybody with a violent streak. Let's refuse him, too."

The two of them had never had so much fun, discussing all the possible young men and listing their good and bad points. Since Kozuru had come into their lives they had not had a single argument. Indeed, they had no time for that.

Kozuru herself had agreed to be adopted. She appeared pleased with the idea and said that she already considered herself a member of Kichizaemon's family. However, there was always that underlying anxiety that her real parents may still be searching for her.

Eight months had passed since she came to live with them, and Kichizaemon believed that sufficient time had elapsed for them to move forward with her adoption. If her real parents were to appear later on, they would have to discuss the situation with them, but in the meantime Kichizaemon and Tomé should relax and choose a suitable husband for her.

Eventually they settled on Hayata Kannosuke, the relative of a retired man called Hayashi who lived in Fukiya and had approached them with the offer. The young man was a skilled swordsman, had done well in his studies, and had an agreeable personality.

"He will make a perfect son," said Hayashi, acting as the intermediary. "As you may know, his family's stipend is only 300 bushels of rice, but I do hope you will overlook this."

Kichizaemon and Tomé talked over the offer with Kozuru and were able to give Hayashi their informal consent. The wedding was set for the autumn, and it was agreed that Kozuru would be officially adopted by Kichizaemon before then so that Kannosuke could enter his family.

Autumn was approaching when Hayashi dispatched a servant to invite Kichizaemon, Tomé, and Kozuru to visit him. He also invited Kannosuke, saying that it would be a good idea for the young man to meet Kozuru over tea. The marriage had been decided and a date set, but neither Tomé nor Kozuru had set eyes on Kannosuke. Only Kichizaemon had met him.

"They were good enough to offer us the opportunity, so I think we should go. I married Tomé without seeing her first, and look what happened to us! If I had met her, I might have turned her down." Kichizaemon smiled as he said this, but in the past that would not have stopped Tomé from hitting back with an insulting rejoinder. Now, however, she simply laughed merrily, and even

Kozuru had trouble hiding a grin. It was only a month before the marriage, and they were all in the best of spirits.

The head of the Hayashi household was the supervisor of the domain's secretarial section. His annual income was 750 bushels of rice, so his house was twice the size of Kichizaemon's. When they arrived, the three guests were led to a room at the rear of the house where Kannosuke was waiting. Although not as good-looking as Hashimoto Sakunosuke, Kichizaemon felt that, if anything, this was a point in his favor.

"He'll make an ideal husband for Kozuru."

Unlike Kichizaemon and Tomé, whose quarrels betrayed a blatant disregard for the rules of polite society, the two young people promised to make a harmonious couple. Kichizaemon was overjoyed at the thought.

After they had left the Hayashi house and were nearing home, Tomé suddenly noticed that Kozuru was looking unwell.

"What's the matter?" Tomé asked, looking anxiously at Kozuru's face as they entered the gate. Kozuru stopped abruptly and covered her face with her hands.

"What's wrong?" Tomé asked again, placing a hand on Kozuru's shoulder and looking uneasily at her husband.

"It is probably the strain," Kichizaemon said as he bent to open the door. "She'll recover once we're indoors and she can rest."

"No," Kozuru said, taking her hands from her face, "it's not that." She had turned deathly white, and beads of perspiration had appeared on her forehead. "I am very sorry," she said, turning to them and speaking firmly, "but you must cancel the marriage."

"Why? Is there something wrong with Kannosuke?"

"It's not that, Father," she answered, her tear-filled eyes fixed on Kichizaemon. "I'm already promised to somebody else."

With that, Kozuru promptly fainted. Tomé uttered a cry and reached out to catch her. Kichizaemon rushed to the unconscious girl's side and helped Tomé carry her into the house.

"This is a fine problem we have."

"Whatever can she be talking about?"

Having put Kozuru to bed, Kichizaemon and Tomé sat in the living room and held a whispered discussion.

"I think it's quite clear. She's remembered her past."

Tomé looked at her husband aghast.

"Will she want to leave us?"

"I don't know. If her memory's come back completely, she may want to leave, but then again she may have some reason not to."

Tomé looked at her husband in silence.

"However, if she has remembered her past and wishes to leave us, we must not try to stop her. First, though, I will have to cancel the marriage. It will be hard on Hayashi and Kannosuke, but it can't be helped."

He realized now that in his eagerness he had allowed himself to get carried away. From the start he had known that there was a chance of something like this happening, but seeing the way Tomé had doted on Kozuru and how Kozuru had reciprocated their affection, calling them "Father" and "Mother," he had let down his guard.

Yet he had to admit he was disappointed at the way things had turned out. If everything had proceeded as planned, he would have had a son to succeed him as head of the household, and his worries about old age would have vanished with a stroke.

"What did she mean when she said she was promised to somebody else?" Tomé asked. She was still dazed and her voice was subdued.

"It means that she has a fiancé or a husband."

"A husband? Kozuru?" Tomé's jaw dropped in shock. "Does that mean she's going to leave us?" she asked again, gazing at Kichizaemon.

"I don't know. We will have to wait and see."

"Well, I don't care if we adopt a son or not, just as long as Kozuru stays with us," Tomé said.

Kichizaemon had to admit that he felt the same way.

Strangely enough, Kozuru soon recovered her spirits and said no more about her past. It had come back to haunt her that one time, and then passed over like a dark cloud.

Kichizaemon broke off the betrothal. Naturally, the Hayata family and Hayashi, the go-between, were most upset, but as Kichizaemon painfully explained the entire situation they realized there was nothing to be done. Kichizaemon and Tomé did not reveal any of this to Kozuru, for their instincts told them it was a subject best left untouched. Kozuru, for her part, said not a word about that day, either. Soon the three of them had settled back into their comfortable relationship.

"That's why I was against rushing things," Kichizaemon said, ignoring the fact that he had been as excited about the betrothal as Tomé. "We must not forget the delicate state she's in. It's best to leave her alone to work this out. We won't know if we've been blessed with a daughter until we know the whole story."

"I agree. I'm happy just to have a daughter in the house. It frightens me to think what would happen if she were to go away and leave us alone again."

The old couple talked in whispers, little realizing that their hopes were about to be shattered.

It was late autumn. The weather was still fine, but the heavy dew in the mornings heralded the approach of winter. One day Kichizaemon returned home from the castle to find visitors waiting for him.

"Who are they?" he asked Tomé, who had met him at the front door looking depressed.

Tomé began to answer, then fell silent, biting her lip.

"What's wrong?"

"They're here for Kozuru."

Kichizaemon entered the house with Tomé behind him.

"They're in Kozuru's room."

There were two visitors, one a tall, well-built young man with firm features, the other a plump, middle-aged man with an open, honest face. Kichizaemon glanced over at Kozuru and felt his heart go out to her. She was sitting slightly apart from the two guests, and it was her face that so moved him. It was exactly the same as on the day he had found her on the bridge. Even when she looked at him, she registered no emotion, and soon her gaze returned to the round window of the room. The rays of the setting sun had tinged everything a deep orange. Kozuru's eyes were vacant, as if she saw nothing.

"My name is Kanna Kichizaemon," he announced, and the two men told him their names and ranks. They had come from the capital of the neighboring domain; the older man was a relative of Kozuru's who worked at the magistrate's office and the young man was the person she was betrothed to. He introduced himself as Terakawa Tozaburo and bowed low before Kichizaemon.

"Your wife has told us the whole story, and I will never forget the great kindness you have shown in looking after Mitsuho."

"Mitsuho?" Kichizaemon looked inquiringly at Tomé.

"Apparently that's her real name," Tomé replied, watching Kozuru's face intently.

The young man explained that Mitsuho had disappeared at the end of July the previous year, immediately after the death of her parents. She had left no note to say where she was going, although she had told her brother and younger sister that she meant to visit their aunt in Edo.

Mitsuho's mother had a sister living in Isshiki in Edo's Fukagawa district. Tozaburo had rushed there on foot, a distance of almost three hundred miles, only to discover that she had never arrived. On his way back he stopped at every town and village to inquire after her, but she seemed to have vanished without a trace.

A year passed with no word of her. Then the magistrate's office in their domain began investigating a robbery that necessitated collaborating with Kichizaemon's domain. The man accompanying Tozaburo was employed in that office, and during the course of inquiries—with officers from both domains visiting back and forth—he heard a rumor that somebody of Mitsuho's description was living in Kichizaemon's care.

"I understand you found her at the beginning of August, so she must have come straight here from home, although I cannot imagine why," Tozaburo remarked.

"I see," Kichizaemon said, looking up. "So do you mean to take her away with you immediately?"

"Yes, if you have no objections. We have already visited the magistrate's office and completed the necessary formalities."

"Naturally I have no objections. Now we know who she is, you must take her with you. It is wonderful news." Then, turning to the older man, he asked if he could have a few moments alone with Tozaburo.

"Of course," the man replied with a cheerful smile that seemed to belie his august position in the magistrate's office. "Take as long as you want."

Kichizaemon left the room, slipped on his sandals, and walked out into the garden, followed by Tozaburo.

"I don't know if you have noticed," he said, turning to the young man, "but Mitsuho or whatever her name is has lost her memory."

A shadow crossed Tozaburo's features for the first time, and he nodded.

"I did notice. She has not said a word to us since we arrived."

"I don't think she's mad. She is just avoiding something that happened in the past."

"I think I know what it is," Tozaburo replied hesitantly.

"I thought you might. Would you tell me about it?"

"I think Mitsuho wants to forget a certain incident."

It appeared that Mitsuho's parents had not died of natural causes. Even though they had three children, they were forever quarreling, and one day in a fit of rage her father had drawn his sword and killed his wife. Realizing what he had done, he had subsequently taken his own life.

"That's the official version of the story as published in the superintendent's report, but the truth is slightly different." Tozaburo paused briefly before continuing. "Apparently, when Mitsuho saw her father kill her mother, she lost control and attacked him with a dagger. The wound was serious, and rather than have his daughter tried for murder, her father had turned his sword on himself to make it look like suicide. At least, that is what I was told in confidence."

Kichizaemon was silent, but he recalled the way Mitsuho had reacted when he and Tomé had started quarreling soon after she came to the house. Watching Tozaburo's face closely, he asked, "And you still intend to take her back?"

"Of course. My main fear was that she had committed suicide somewhere, without anybody knowing. It's enough for me to know she is alive. I will take her back and care for her until she recovers. I believe she is not beyond help."

"She has been happy living here."

Tozaburo lowered his head in thought, then he looked up and spoke confidently. "I think that was probably because she did not have to face up to what she had done. However, that is not a true cure. The only way she can fully recover is to confront her deed and overcome the pain by herself."

"I agree." Kichizaemon spoke firmly. He realized that this man could be trusted to act correctly, and clasped his hand warmly. "Please look after her. I'm sure you are the right person for her and the only one capable of seeing her cured."

Tozaburo turned back toward the house.

"And who was Kozuru?" Kichizaemon added in a low voice.

"That was her mother's name."

A short while later Kichizaemon and Tomé stood by the gate and watched as Tozaburo led Mitsuho away by the hand. Seeing her pale face and withdrawn expression, Tomé called out, "Mitsuho, look after yourself!"

Mitsuho did not turn around.

"That's enough," Kichizaemon said, but Tomé could not stop herself. She called out one last time, in a tear-choked voice.

"Kozuru!"

This time Mitsuho stopped, and as she looked back a faint emotion seemed to flit across her features. She bowed deeply to them. Then, gripping Tozaburo's hand, she turned and walked away.

After that, the sound of quarrels could occasionally be heard coming from Kichizaemon's house, but they had none of their old vigor. And all talk of young men willing to be adopted into the family ceased completely.

Shinza, the Samurai

Jibu Shinza was easily the most unpopular man in the whole domain. As chief guard of the daimyo's battle standard, he was required to be at his post in the castle keep every day. If he was in a good mood, he would regale his subordinates with boastful tales of the numerous battles he had fought when young, but as they had heard them all before it was a struggle for them to stifle their yawns and look attentive. On days when Shinza was not feeling talkative, he simply sat in stony silence in front of the battle standard until it was time to go home. One might say that his was not a demanding job.

The fall of Osaka Castle in the summer of 1615 and the ensuing rout of the armies loyal to the son of Toyotomi Hideyoshi, the old dictator, had brought peace to the country for the first time in almost one and a half centuries. But for men like Shinza, who had been raised in a climate of war, the monotony of the new era was almost intolerable.

The changing times ushered in new priorities, and the number of guards for the battle standard was gradually decreased. By the time Shinza had been appointed chief in 1620—seven years ago—only thirteen samurai remained. The battle standard was kept in a large chest in a room of its own, and each day two members of the guard would be on duty with Shinza, leaving the others free to do whatever they liked. Every six months the battle standard and other war emblems of the clan were taken out of their storage boxes to be aired and checked for any necessary repairs, but as this was the extent of their duties, there was no call for more guards. The room the battle standard was kept in had a single north-facing window that let in little light, and Shinza would sit in silence in the semi-darkness the whole day, seldom venturing out at all.

Shinza's unpopularity stemmed from the fact that he seemed to delight in being perverse. Even the simplest greeting would be met by some sarcastic retort, and when people crossed his path on their way to the castle, they would invariably grimace. Some even looked around desperately for an avenue of escape, but he was an officer and therefore not to be ignored.

"A fine day, is it not?" they might say, choosing the least controversial opening.

"For the moment. But look at those clouds. I would not be surprised if we saw rain by the afternoon." He enjoyed contradicting whatever anyone said, which annoyed people no end—and this was in a mere exchange of greetings. A longer conversation or a discussion would regularly result in the other person losing his temper. So it was not at all surprising that he had become so disliked, yet his reputation did not bother him in the least.

Shinza had a rugged face, with a square jaw, sunken cheeks, and heavy eyebrows protruding aggressively over large, bulging eyes. As he strode purposefully between the castle and his home in Jizo, he generally kept his eyes fixed firmly on the ground.

Despite his unpopularity, no one could deny his courage as a warrior. Shinza had taken part in his first battle at the age of eighteen, had sailed to Korea with Hideyoshi's armies in 1592, and had fought at the great Battle of Sekigahara in 1600 that had confirmed Tokugawa Ieyasu as shogun. He had also been present at both sieges of Osaka Castle, winning acclaim for his martial skills as a member of the old daimyo's bodyguard.

The daimyo had kept Shinza by his side because of his mastery of the martial arts. During the final battle at Osaka, when the enemy managed to break through the lines and headed straight for the battle standard, many had seen the lone figure of Shinza keeping the soldiers at bay with his sword. In the ten years since that battle most of the people who had witnessed his exploits had died, leaving only rumors of his past acts of valor. However, one person at least had not forgotten them.

"Sir, please come quickly. It's an emergency!" cried a young samurai, rushing into the battle standard room. Shinza stared hard at him until the young man remembered his manners and dropped to his knees. "There's a fight going on inside the castle, sir. Please come."

"Who is fighting?"

"I'm not sure.

"You're not sure? You come rushing in to ask for my help without even finding out who's involved?" Shinza's tone dripped with scorn, but he rose to his feet with an alacrity belying his fifty-eight years. He ordered the other two guards to remain where they were and hurried outside.

"Where are they?"

"In the garden of the Kashoden." The Kashoden was a building on the southern edge of the castle containing a stage for Nō drama and a library, but people seldom went there. The building was set in a small garden that had been landscaped with diminutive hills, streams, and ponds that created a great feeling of space. They arrived to find a young man with his sword drawn standing with his back to a stone lantern in the small hollow below an artificial hill. His face was pale and he was shouting incoherently. His opponent, facing away from Shinza, was a tall samurai whose sword remained sheathed. Surrounding them were some twenty samurai.

"Shinoi, put your sword away!" cried one of them.

"Don't do anything rash! Remember where you are!" exhorted another.

The bystanders were trying to persuade the two combatants to break off the fight, although none tried to intervene. The sword blade glinted coldly in the morning sun. Each time it moved, the circle of spectators drew back.

So the one brandishing the sword was called Shinoi, Shinza thought. He wondered if he was related to the chamberlain, Shinoi Ukyo, one of the most powerful men in the domain. The young man looked very tense and nervous; his thin face was pale and his eyes were bloodshot.

"Sheathe your sword! We're in the castle," said his opponent.

"If you want to fight, let's abide by the rules and go outside. Can't you understand what I'm saying?"

"Coward!" Shinoi Shumé screamed. "Enough talk! Draw your sword! Are you scared because we're in the castle? I'm not."

"Don't be a fool! Control yourself!" The man with his back to Shinza spoke in a calm, relaxed tone.

Just a minute, that sounds like the boy next door, Shinza thought, suddenly recognizing the voice. He had seen enough to realize that the man waving the sword was hysterical and unable to listen to reason, while his opponent, empty-handed but completely relaxed, was none other than Inukai Heishiro, his neighbor's eldest son. Shinza had occasionally caught him looking over the hedge between their gardens and exchanging pleasantries with his daughter, Yoshie. The previous autumn Heishiro's father, Gunbei, had collapsed in the castle and had been confined to his bed ever since, so from the beginning of January Heishiro had taken over as head of the family. He had assumed his post in the bodyguard only two months ago, in February.

It hadn't taken long for the foolish boy to get himself into trouble, thought Shinza. When he had caught Heishiro talking to his daughter in the garden, the young man had seemed unperturbed and had offered him a casual greeting, quite indifferent to Shinza's glare. He had then bid Yoshie goodbye in a voice so gentle that it made the hairs on Shinza's neck stand up. Shinza was annoyed with Yoshie for even deigning to talk to such an impudent fellow, but he had not said anything. He could never bring himself to rebuke her, no matter what she did.

Yoshie was eighteen years old, and she was such a beauty that people found it difficult to believe she could really be Shinza's daughter. Despite her good looks, though, nobody had approached him for her hand. Being an only child, her eventual husband stood to inherit her father's wealth and position. There were any number of second or third sons with no future prospects of their own, but none seemed willing to marry her. Even if a suitable match was suggested, nothing ever came of it because as soon as Shinza's name was mentioned, the potential son-in-law would get cold feet. Shinza was only just beginning to realize that his reputation might stand in the way of his daughter's marital happiness, and he felt obligated to do something for her. To complicate matters Shinza had lost his wife two years earlier, and although he had a maid and a servant, it was Yoshie who managed the household, so he owed her for that, too. However, one day soon he was determined to give Heishiro a piece of his mind.

Be that as it may, he could not stand idly by and watch Heishiro be killed. The thought of how much this might upset Yoshie did cross his mind, although he did not like to dwell on the reasons why. He could see the danger Heishiro was in, even if the young man himself appeared oblivious to it.

"Step back, Heishiro," Shinza ordered.

At the moment Shinza spoke, Shinoi Shumé lashed out with his sword. His rage lent power to the stroke, and Heishiro only narrowly dodged the blade. The crowd of spectators moved back as Heishiro put his hand on his sword hilt, realizing that now he had no option but to fight. Shinoi prepared to strike a second time, but as he did so Shinza stepped in between the two. Shinoi paused to size up his new opponent, then bringing his sword tip down to the level of Shinza's eyes, he began to inch backward.

Shinza stepped forward quickly to prevent him from launching another attack. He had not drawn his own sword and his movements seemed almost offhand, but even so beads of sweat appeared on Shinoi's forehead. It was obvious that Shinza's mere presence was enough to unnerve the younger man. In the end, Shinoi's retreat was cut off by the stone lantern. With eyes bulging, and shaking with rage or fear, Shinoi leaped to one side and raised his sword to strike the older man. Just as he did so, a terrifying shout issued from Shinza's mouth.

"Yaaa-aah!"

Paralyzed by that terrible cry, Shinoi fell to his knees. Shinza knocked the sword from his hand, and seizing him by the collar punched him in the face. Shinoi seemed incapable of movement and merely looked blankly at Shinza.

Shinoi was apparently not the only one to have been immobilized by the cry. The onlookers were equally stunned, and some appeared on the verge of collapse. The shout had been so powerful that it made their guts churn.

Watched by all in silence, Shinza made his way back to the castle keep. There he removed his muddied socks, and holding them in one hand he disappeared down the corridor toward his post.

"So that is what is meant by *kiai-jutsu*," one of the bystanders muttered, naming the martial art in which a shout is used to disable and confuse an opponent.

Shinza was looking surly.

Heishiro had come over to his house with some of his mother's pickles to thank him for his help the previous day. The pickles were a favorite of Shinza's, and having saved the young man's life, he felt he was entitled to them. However, he had not expected Heishiro to have the audacity to remove his shoes and step inside the house. It was not as though Shinza had invited him in. Although Heishiro's pleasant appearance made a good impression, Shinza had always felt that he was really a crafty, lazy young man, and he could never fathom what he was thinking. Naturally, he would not dream of asking him into his house. So imagine his shock when Yoshie did just that.

To his horror, Heishiro had the presumption to accept her invitation without a moment's thought. In Shinza's opinion, Heishiro should simply have paid his respects at the front door, given Shinza the pickles, made his excuses, and left. That is what samurai etiquette dictated. What other business could he have here?

Moreover, his behavior after entering the living room exceeded all bounds of decency. When Yoshie came in with a tray of green tea, Heishiro promptly stood up and walked over to the veranda, where he complimented her on the garden, remarking that this part of it was not visible from his house and asking her the names of the various trees.

Yoshie's own behavior was no better. She abandoned all discretion, turning her back on her father and going to stand next to the man, answering his questions animatedly. They behaved as though he was not there, or so it appeared to him. When he cleared his throat, they turned hurriedly, as though noticing his presence for the first time.

"Please excuse me," Heishiro said, with complete composure. At least Yoshie had the decency to blush and look embarrassed, but this did not stop her following Heishiro back into the room. Glancing down at the tray she had brought, Shinza noticed that there were three cups, and he realized that she was intending to join them for tea.

What does she think she's doing? Shinza pondered, looking even surlier. Despite Yoshie's youth, she was now the woman of the house, so he could not just order her out of the room.

"That was an amazing shout yesterday. Was it *kiai-jutsu*?" Heishiro asked.

An amazing shout? Shinza thought. There must be a better way of describing it! He sat with a scowl on his face and did not answer.

"What shout?" Yoshie asked.

"As I was telling you, I almost got into a sword fight with Shinoi Shumé, but then your father appeared and let out a bloodcurdling yell."

"Oh," Yoshie said, her face turning crimson. "I hope he didn't make a fool of himself. You know how he is."

That was quite uncalled for, Shinza thought. When I was a boy, nobody would have been surprised by a shout like that. Young people today have never known battle, so they collapse in fright at the slightest noise and make a big fuss about it. Some even claimed it had been wrong of him to punch Shinoi, but that was ridiculous. When he was young, punishment like that was the norm. In those days violence may have been more common, but at least people had better manners.

"Then your father hit Shinoi so hard that his cheek will be swollen for at least a week."

"Poor man," Yoshie said with a giggle. Heishiro responded with a grin. Shinza cleared his throat again.

"Excuse me," Heishiro said, sitting up straight as etiquette required when talking to an older and more senior man.

"Tell me something," Shinza said. "I have yet to learn the cause of the fight. It must have been something quite exceptional for Shinoi to have drawn his sword inside the castle."

"It wasn't really," Heishiro said, scratching his head in sudden embarrassment. "It all started with a silly argument."

"I see—a silly argument," Shinza repeated, nodding in exaggerated understanding, his every word heavy with sarcasm. "I must say you young people are braver than we were in my time. We were always fearful of drawing our swords inside the castle because it was a capital offense. However, if a fight did start we would not send for anyone to break it up."

"That's why I told Shinoi not to draw his sword. But he was out of control," Heishiro replied blithely, oblivious to Shinza's sarcasm.

"Are the two of you on bad terms?"

"No, I wouldn't go that far," Heishiro said with a smile. He paused, obviously considering whether to continue or not. "Let's just say that we've had our misunderstandings."

"I regret that I don't comprehend your meaning," Shinza said, a dangerous gleam in his eyes. "Friends do not fight, yet when I ask if you are on bad terms, you answer no. You'd better tell me about these misunderstandings."

"Father!" Yoshie exclaimed, glaring at him. "Heishiro obviously does not want to talk about it, so you should not tease him like that!"

"Humph," Shinza snorted, his bulging eyes sparkling and a smile forming on his lips. He had put Heishiro in a spot and was determined to derive as much enjoyment from it as possible. After all, it was for Yoshie's good that he should show up this infuriating young man for what he was.

"That's precisely why I asked. If he is not willing to talk about it, then it must involve a woman. Such misunderstandings always do and always will." He grinned broadly. "Correct me if I'm wrong!"

"Father! Don't be so vulgar," Yoshie said, burying her face in her hands. "You're embarrassing me."

"Don't upset yourself, Yoshie," Heishiro said soothingly. "Your father's mistaken, but the matter is a delicate one and I would rather discuss it with him alone."

Uncovering her face, Yoshie gave him a stern look, which made him quickly wave his hand in a gesture of denial.

"Don't get me wrong. This has nothing to do with a woman."

Don't me wrong? What's that supposed to mean! thought Shinza, making an irritated click with his tongue. To hear the two of them talk, anyone would think they were committed to each other in some way! At this idea he gave a sudden start and looked at them with fresh eyes. Were their affections reciprocated? Yoshie certainly seemed to look on Heishiro with a certain fondness.

He knew the Inukai family had two sons and one daughter. Heishiro was the eldest child, followed by a girl named Saku, and then young Gennosuke, who was still a boy attending the samurai school. However, he knew nothing about any of them. He remembered that Heishiro had been a rather unruly youth, who was always crawling through a gap in the garden hedge to pick the chrysanthemums that his late wife had cultivated with such care. When Gunbei had fallen ill and Heishiro took over as head of the household, Shinza had been surprised to learn that the boy was already an adult.

He had no idea of what had passed between his daughter and Heishiro over the years, but if they did care for each other, it would be a problem. As the eldest son, Heishiro was duty-bound to become the head of his family, while Yoshie as an only daughter was obliged to find a husband willing to be adopted into Shinza's family and take the Jibu name. Even worse, though, was the thought that this confident, arrogant young man might have won his daughter's affections.

Yoshie left the room, and Shinza immediately turned to Heishiro.

"How old are you?" he asked abruptly.

"Twenty-five."

Shinza saw that he was right to be suspicious. Twenty-five and eighteen—they were at just the right ages to consider marriage. He cursed himself for not realizing what had been going on under his very nose.

"You are not married?"

Heishiro looked surprised but responded frankly. "No. Nobody considered me mature enough for marriage, so there has been no talk of it."

"I'm glad you see the problem."

Heishiro gave a wry grin but did not seem upset. Shinza was disappointed. A comment like that would usually anger people, and if their tempers were short they might even storm out of the room. With Heishiro, however, his insults seemed like wasted arrows, falling to the ground before they reached their mark. It was all most unsatisfactory.

"To return to the other subject . . ." Heishiro said, speaking gravely.

Shinza looked at him blankly.

"The reason for the argument with Shinoi Shumé."

"Oh yes."

Shinza had lost interest in that, but having brought it up in the first place, he had no choice but to listen.

"It concerns my sister, Saku."

"You mean he tried to force himself on her?"

"If that were the case, things would be much simpler. No, Shinoi Shumé was acting like a common pimp."

"Oh?"

Apparently, six months earlier, Shinoi Ukyo, the clan chamberlain, had approached the Inukai family and virtually ordered them to present Saku for service at the castle. The Inukai family had refused because it was rumored that the reason the chamberlain was so eager for daughters of clan retainers to work inside the castle was so that he could offer the girls to the daimyo, Nobutaka. Indeed, at least three families had received remarkably rapid promotions after their daughters had been summoned to the lord's bedchamber.

Nobutaka was not half the man that his father, the previous daimyo Mitsuyoshi, had been and Ukyo used such tactics to curry favor with him while simultaneously strengthening his own ties with the families whose daughters had become the lord's mistresses, thereby creating a tightly knit clique within the clan.

The Inukai family had too much pride to seek promotion in this way, but Ukyo took their refusal as a personal insult and worked vindictively through the family's superiors and relatives to bend them to his will. It was while Heishiro's father was having an argument about this with Mikami Hachirozaemon, a high-ranking relative, that he had suffered his stroke. Mikami had once been a councilor, and since his youngest daughter had been selected as one of the daimyo's mistresses, he enjoyed a particularly close relationship with Ukyo.

After Heishiro took over as head of the family, Ukyo had continued to press him on the subject, but Heishiro had naturally rejected all such approaches, which led indirectly to the confrontation with Shinoi Shumé, Ukyo's nephew.

Heishiro had been walking through the castle grounds that day when he met Shinoi coming the other way. As they passed each other, Shinoi had given a scornful laugh and said, "Some people are so pig-headed they cannot recognize good fortune even when it's staring them in the face." Shinoi often took advantage of his uncle's position to behave in such a high-handed, overbearing manner. Fortunately, he and Heishiro worked in different sections and had little contact.

"What did you say?" Heishiro had asked. "Oh, it's you, the nephew of the old pimp."

This had led to the scene in the garden.

"You really said that?" Shinza snorted, warming to the young man a little.

"Yes."

"I apologize. I had not realized the position you were in. It must be hard for you." He was tempted to add that, given Heishiro's new duties, he was surprised the young man could find the time to hang around Yoshie so much, but he managed to resist. He had always considered Heishiro thoughtless and impudent, but the way the young man was dealing with his problems without complaint deserved grudging admiration.

A wave of disgust and loathing against Shinoi Ukyo suddenly swept over him. He took no interest in clan politics, but he was well aware of what Ukyo had been up to all these years.

"Since Lord Mitsuyoshi's time, Shinoi Ukyo has been burrowing into the clan hierarchy like a rat—and a dirty one at that. He rose to power when he prostituted himself to the young lord, Nobutaka, when he was still a child."

"I see."

"His methods have not changed, only now that he is old and nobody wants his body, he procures young women instead."

"Actually, it's not only women he procures."

As Heishiro said this, they heard Yoshie call from the corridor outside.

"May I come in?"

"Yes," Shinza replied. As she entered the room, the two men exchanged embarrassed looks. Their discussion had been of indelicate matters and their voices a shade too loud. However, Yoshie's face betrayed no sign that she had overheard.

"You must stay and have a meal with us, Heishiro. There's no need for you to hurry home," Yoshie said cheerfully.

It was because she said things like this that Heishiro took advantage of her, thought Shinza, turning away with a grimace. After their conversation, he had begun to consider Heishiro in a new light, but he reminded himself that he was the same impudent young man as always. He certainly did not want to have to eat with him.

"Thank you, Yoshie," Heishiro said, "but it's my first visit to your house and I have already stayed too long. I'll be reprimanded by my parents if I don't return soon."

I should think so, Shinza thought with relief. Turning to look at them again, he noticed that the light that had been flooding into the room earlier had now dimmed into twilight.

Yoshie sounded disappointed as she said, "In that case you must come again so that I can prepare a proper meal."

Now why did she have to say that? Shinza thought. It's not as if she's going to marry him. I don't want the neighbor's boy hanging around here all the time. He may have felt in my debt, but he's thanked me now. There's no need for any more dealings.

"Don't you agree, Father?" Yoshie asked, turning to him. "Isn't it regrettable that he has to leave."

"Hmm," Shinza murmured noncommittally, although he hated himself for doing so. He did not think it regrettable in the least.

Yoshie lit the lamp in the room and left to make more tea.

"About Ukyo procuring girls," Heishiro started.

"Yes?" Shinza was saying as little as possible. He was fed up and reproached himself for having let the boy come into the house. He had never guessed it would be so difficult to be rid of him.

"Over the years, Ukyo has done more harm than just procuring girls for the daimyo. His policies have all been utter failures, too."

"What do you mean?" Shinza asked, despite his lack of interest in politics.

"You know the area around Mount Inami that was declared a hunting reserve six years ago."

"Yes."

Heishiro was referring to the low hills about five miles south of the town. It was a densely wooded area with deep valleys, and few people lived in it. When Shinza was younger, he had occasionally gone hunting there when he was not on duty, but he had not visited it since it was declared a reserve.

"Did you hear that fifteen farmers from Mitsukama village disappeared?"

"No, but what's the connection between the farmers and Mount Inami?"

Deep in the heart of the Inami area was a ravine known as Gojindani. It resembled a huge rock that had been cleft in two by elemental forces, and a dark stream ran along its base. This valley was famous for the gold dust that could be found there, but during the last five or six years the source had been exhausted. Ukyo had been in charge of extracting the gold and had ordered farmers from Mitsukama village to be used for the work.

"The gold was sold to brokers in Osaka. Ukyo gave some of the proceeds to Chief Councilor Shiino to buy his silence and kept the rest for himself. But there is some mystery concerning the farmers. They were reported to have fled because they could not pay the tithes on their land, but none of them has ever been seen again. The truth is that they were the ones who extracted the gold, and after the work was finished it is believed that they were either transported out of the domain or killed on Ukyo's orders."

"You seem very well informed." Shinza was forced once more to revise his opinion of the young man. There was no denying his impertinence, but he was obviously not stupid. He was alert to important matters and might even be described as possessing some judgment.

However, Heishiro's next comment shattered this impression.

"Actually, I heard all this from Vice Councilor Kato," he said, scratching his head in embarrassment.

"Kato? You mean Kato Zusho?"

Kato Zusho was vice councilor to the daimyo, although the actual running of the domain was handled by Chief Councilor Shiino Hikobei and Chamberlain Shinoi Ukyo. They were assisted by Councilor Yamagata Takizo and Lieutenant Akamatsu Chuta, a very able man who was expected to take over from Ukyo in the future. This meant that Kato Zusho was sidelined, and in the last two years he had hardly set foot in the castle, preferring to remain on his estate.

Heishiro went on to explain that Kato Zusho's retreat from politics had been voluntary. Shinoi Ukyo, Yamagata, and Akamatsu had succeeded in taking over the daily management of the domain and although nominally Ukyo's superior, Chief Councilor Shiino had accepted so many bribes that he no longer had any power over him. Ukyo had even tried to bribe Kato, offering him a luxurious villa he had built on the western fringes of the Inami area, but Kato had refused it, leading to a growing hostility between the two and Kato's ultimate withdrawal from clan politics.

"However, Vice Councilor Kato believes that Ukyo's tyranny can no longer be ignored," Heishiro continued. "An increasing number of people in the clan feel it's time to end the high-handedness of the Shinoi faction."

"And I take it you're one of them."

"Naturally," Heishiro replied proudly. He sounded cheerful, and his lack of concern about the outcome was an attitude befitting a samurai. Despite that, Heishiro's garrulousness lowered him somewhat in Shinza's estimate.

"I believe I have a good idea of what's happening, but don't you think you're being a little rash in revealing it to me? What if I were to tell Shinoi Ukyo? If word got out that Kato was creating a faction of his own, it could destroy him."

"I'm not worried about that," Heishiro replied calmly. "I know you're not the kind of man to betray us."

"You can't be sure. I have no friends or enemies among the clan's upper echelons, but even I must admit to being a little perverse at times."

"You mean that you are going to tell Ukyo?" Heishiro asked, suddenly reaching for his sword, which was lying on the floor beside him.

"Fool! Put it down," Shinza barked. He was disgusted. He had given this man a cup of tea and now he was going to start swinging his sword around. He could not understand young people any more. First Heishiro revealed a dangerous secret to him, then as soon as Shinza made a small joke, he went for his sword.

When younger, Shinza had fought against the Koreans, but he understood Heishiro no better than he had them.

"Do you really believe I am like that?" he asked with a sigh.

"No, as I said earlier, I have always held you in the highest respect and I don't think there's another samurai in the domain who can rival your integrity."

Now he's flattering me, thought Shinza, displeased. He just could not figure out the boy. If he respects me so much, why does he keep flirting with Yoshie and giggling when their eyes meet, as if I were not there?

"I'd like to ask you a favor," Heishiro said.

"What now?" Shinza replied, his ill-temper evident in his tone.

"I'd like you to meet Vice Councilor Kato."

At that moment the door slid open and Yoshie reentered. She had brought not only freshly made tea but a plate of exquisite-looking cakes. That explained why she had been gone so long, Shinza thought. Only one place in town sold such cakes, so she must have sent the maid to buy them. And they weren't cheap.

Yoshie served the two men and Shinza noticed that she had given Heishiro one cake more than him, which did nothing to improve his temper.

"Sorry, but that is out of the question."

Heishiro could not hide his disappointment. "Actually, the vice councilor himself asked me to try to persuade you."

"Kato Zusho asked that?"

"Yes. He said that if you joined our side, that alone would be worth a hundred men."

"Not surprising! They're a spineless bunch, yet you say that you're one of them. I won't join any petty faction. Shi—" Shinza was about to mention Shinoi's name, but seeing that Yoshie was following their conversation with a suspicious expression, he broke off. "If you ask me, it would only take one skilled swordsman to sort the whole thing out."

"Is that your final word?"

"Yes. Anyway, Kato Zusho already owes me a favor. Tell him that if he wants to ask for another, he should do so in a more civil way. That's all I have to say."

Shinza rose to his feet, saying, "Yoshie, Heishiro is ready to leave."

"I'll just finish these cakes, if I may," Heishiro said, and Yoshie hurriedly poured him another cup of tea. Shinza could hardly believe his ears. As he stood up to leave the room, he paused at the door, struck by a thought.

"How old did you say Saku was?"

Heishiro was hurriedly trying to swallow his cake, so Yoshie answered instead.

"She's fourteen."

Shinza slid open one of the papered doors facing the garden and looked out into the darkness. The night breeze carried the scent of new foliage.

"She was fourteen, too," he muttered, the mention of Kato Zusho's name evoking an old memory. The face of a young foreign girl appeared before him, and he peered harder into the darkness as though to see her more clearly.

Shortly after six in the evening, Shinza walked through the deserted castle grounds toward the main gate on his way home.

Kato Zusho had made a rare appearance at the castle that day and had met with various people. A short while before four o'clock, as everybody was preparing to go home, he called unexpectedly at Shinza's post. The two talked, but Kato had little to add to what Shinza had already heard from Heishiro. After outlining events in the domain, he politely asked Shinza to join his faction.

"Shinoi Ukyo has a large following so we need as many as we can muster if we are to defeat him." He then listed the powerful figures who shared his views, such as the former chief councilor, Naganuma Tarozaemon, Councilor Hoshina Rinya, who was in charge of agricultural policy and independent of Shinoi, and Chief Censor Handa Sakubei. Kato believed that they had gathered enough evidence to present to the daimyo in order to force Shinoi Ukyo out.

"That seems a very circuitous way of doing things," Shinza said. "Why go to all that trouble? If you can prove he's no good, all you have to do is . . ." He made a chopping motion with his hand.

"I don't want any blood spilled," Kato replied calmly. "We cannot afford any semblance of a rebellion." He was obviously worried about the central government in distant Edo. Ever since the Tokugawa family came to power after the Battle of Sekigahara in 1600, the government had made it a policy to disband as many clans as possible. Among the excuses used for this was the lack of an heir upon the death of a daimyo or the construction of illegal fortifications in a castle, but rebellion was also a common justification.

In 1618 two daimyo had lost their domains as punishment for an insurrection by their followers, and in 1621 the powerful Mogami family that ruled much of northern Japan lost its fief when it was discovered that an insurrection had taken place during the rule of the previous daimyo. The list of dispersed clans was long, and it was obvious that the government intended to strengthen its position by breaking up all the clans with no long-standing relationship with the Tokugawa family.

"Won't you help us?" Even though Kato spoke calmly, his ambition was evident in his tone.

They are two of a kind, Shinza thought. When he had first heard about all this from Heishiro, he had realized that Kato Zusho simply wanted to take over the running of the clan and was using Shinoi Ukyo's failures as an excuse to increase his own influence. The obvious care with which he was planning his moves proved his intentions.

Kato is not half the man Heishiro takes him for, he thought. His mind went back to an event on a foreign battlefield forty years earlier, when he and Kato had held the same rank in the bodyguard. At that time Kato had stolen a young woman from him and offered her to the daimyo.

"I'll never join you," Shinza said decisively.

"Are you still angry with me after all these years?" Kato asked with a strange smile on his face that could be taken for either commiseration or contempt.

"Yes, I am. I'll never throw in my lot with you."

Shinza spoke as if to an equal. Although the Kato family was one of the oldest and most powerful in the clan, it had fallen on hard times when Zusho was a young man. He had enlisted in the bodyguard, just as Shinza had done. However, politics ran in Zusho's blood, and he displayed such talent for it that by the time Lord Mitsuyoshi died he had secured the post of vice councilor, with an annual stipend of 5,000 bushels of rice. There was now a huge gap between his position and that of the chief guard of the battle standard, which only commanded an income of 550 bushels of rice.

"Help me, for old time's sake."

"Never. I'm no fool. I know you just want to take Shinoi's place."

"You never change, do you? Always so contrary," Kato said with a wry smile. And who made me that way? Shinza thought, but did not say anything. Anyway, Kato would never understand.

"Well," Kato said, rising and walking toward the door. "You have as good as joined my faction anyway."

"What do you mean?"

"A lot of people saw me come in here, and some will surely conclude that you're backing me."

Shinza said nothing.

"You'll have to choose eventually, and it is my star that is rising. The clan is split, and I have all the evidence I need to prove Shinoi's corruption, so I am in the stronger position. It is in your own interest to make up your mind soon."

"Loathsome creature," Shinza muttered as he hurried across the courtyard. Suddenly a voice called out to him.

"Uncle Jibu!"

A small white face was staring at him out of the darkness beside the gate, beyond the reach of the guard's torches. A hand beckoned.

Shinza felt a spasm of fear run through him. A moment before he had been cursing Kato Zusho as a badger, fox, or some other beast of evil omen, and now a real one was calling to him!

"Uncle Jibu, over here!" The hand beckoned once again. Drawing closer, he saw the crouching figure of a young girl in a white kimono. As he approached, she stood up and he was shocked to see who it was.

"Why, it's Saku. What on earth are you doing here?"

It was Heishiro's younger sister. She was learning sewing from Yoshie and often came to his house, so he recognized her immediately.

"Uncle, can you please help me escape from the castle?" she asked, putting her hands together in supplication.

"Of course. But that looks like a nightdress. What are you doing dressed like that?" His tone was severe, but looking at her pale face and noticing the way she was biting her lip in fear, the truth suddenly dawned on him.

This is Shinoi Ukyo's doing, he thought.

"Put this on," he said in a gentler voice than he had used for years, giving her his jacket. "There's nothing to be afraid of now."

They walked out of the castle keep and through the inner bailey. They made an unlikely couple, but though the guards were surprised the look on Shinza's face discouraged all questions.

After they had left the castle grounds, Shinza stopped and asked, "Are you cold?"

"No, thank you," Saku answered politely. All at once she buried her face in his chest and burst into tears, the intensity of her sobs revealing the emotion she had been keeping in check.

"Come, come, you're a samurai girl, so you mustn't cry like that. Tell me what happened," Shinza said, patting her on the shoulder. The slenderness of her body reminded him that she was still little more than a child. His rage against Shinoi Ukyo continued to build up inside him.

As they walked back toward her house, Saku told him everything that had happened, and it was much as he had suspected.

That afternoon she had been invited to a party held by the Mikamis for their daughter. Since the Mikamis were relatives, as well as the head of the extended family, nobody suspected anything untoward. After the party, Saku had dinner at the house and then boarded a palanquin to go home. The Mikamis were wealthy so it was not unusual that they would go to the expense of ordering a palanquin specially for her. However, when the palanquin arrived at its destination, she found she was inside the castle.

Three ladies-in-waiting rushed out and led the girl through to the private apartments, bathed her, applied makeup, and put her in a nightdress. It was not until after she found herself inside what she assumed was the daimyo's bedchamber that she found a chance to escape.

As Saku recounted this to Shinza, she occasionally broke down and sobbed, covering her face with her hands. The night was dark, with only the light of the stars to guide them, but when he looked down on the whiteness of her neck as she bowed her head, his thoughts went back to the girl he had met on foreign soil forty years before. In his mind, Shinoi Ukyo replaced Kato Zusho as the man who had stolen her from him and offered her to the daimyo in order to gain favor.

It had happened in Korea in May 1592. Shinza's brigade had marched from Pusan over the Sobaek-Sanmaek mountains to their billet in a village by the Kum River. Shinza was twenty years old at the time. The soldiers under Lord Mitsuyoshi's command were functioning as a rearguard for the armies under Kuroda Nagamasa and Otomo Yoshimune, who had landed at Kimhae and were moving toward the capital, Hanyang. The original plan had been to follow the two armies to Hanyang, but enemy activity at the rear had changed that and Shinza's brigade was held in readiness for a counterattack from that direction.

The village where Shinza's brigade was stationed was on top of a hill overlooking the eastern bank of the river. The village was deserted as all the inhabitants had fled. As the sun dipped toward the distant mountains, the light turned the river into a ribbon of silver, and magpies circling above scolded the Japanese invaders.

As the Korean army had not yet been sighted, Lord Mitsuyoshi and his corps of three hundred samurai had a lot of time on their hands and not much to do. One day Shinza wandered into an abandoned farmhouse lying at the edge of the village. It was enclosed by mud walls, over which hung the low branches of a jujube tree. Japanese troops had clearly been there before, for one of its walls had been knocked in and the door broken. Unripe peaches from a tree lay shriveling in the garden.

It was here that he found the girl. She was hiding under a pile of straw in a storeroom. He wondered why she had not fled with the rest of her family, but soon discovered that she had been wounded in the thigh by a spear, and the wound had become infected.

When Shinza saw the girl, he experienced an emotion akin to dismay. His immediate reaction was to keep her concealed by any means and not let anyone know of her existence. The five rotting corpses of villagers he had seen when he had reached the village, as well as the wanton damage to the houses, were all evidence that the Japanese army had passed through. He knew that it would only take one small incident to turn three hundred bored soldiers into a mob, and he decided he could not allow the girl to be seen.

He hurried out of the farmhouse to make sure no one was about, then went back to attend to the girl's injury. Her arms and legs were emaciated, and at a guess he did not think she was more than ten years old. Shinza sucked the puss from her pale thigh and washed it with water from the garden well. He then applied some ointment. The girl watched the entire procedure with a vacant expression on her face, and when he touched her forehead he realized that she was running a fever.

"Don't be afraid. I'll bring you some food when it's dark." He smiled as he spoke, but the girl lay there motionless, watching him in silence. He covered her with the straw again and returned to the village.

That night he came back with some food for her, a rice ball.

She was too weak to eat by herself, so he chewed the rice to soften it before placing it in her mouth with his finger. All she could manage at first was a few grains of rice, but as she remembered the taste of food, she began to chew while sucking at his finger. Finally, she revived enough to bite his finger weakly.

Shinza continued feeding the girl for ten days, and during this time her dry, scaly skin regained some of its luster. Although her arms and legs were still scrawny, her cheeks took on a little color and her dark eyes began to sparkle. She never said a word, but when she looked at Shinza there was the hint of a smile.

One night, as he was about to leave, she raised herself up and, seizing his arm, said something rapidly. Losing his balance, Shinza fell on top of her but leaped back up as quickly as if he had touched a flame. As he had put his arm out to break his fall, his hand had touched a well-formed breast. However, the girl would not let go of him and pointed repeatedly to the pile of straw next to her. Soft moonlight flooded in through the window.

Shinza shook his head and freed himself from her grip. As he left the room, he could feel his heart pounding, but the moment he came into the garden, he froze. There was a man standing there, and as he drew closer he saw that it was Ko, a Korean man in his thirties they were using as an interpreter.

"Did you see her?"

"Yes," Ko replied. Although his face was clearly visible in the moonlight, Shinza could not read his expression.

"She was wounded and was hiding in there. I looked after her and she's getting better." As he spoke he realized that Ko would never understand his feelings toward the girl. To Ko, he was simply a Japanese soldier who was keeping a village girl as a mistress. Shinza knew no words to convince him otherwise.

"Don't tell anyone. If they find her, she'll be raped."

"I understand," Ko responded meekly.

An idea suddenly occurred to Shinza.

"Can you ask her name and age?"

Ko entered the farmhouse, and at the sight of him the girl sat bolt upright. There followed a brief but rapid exchange, but Shinza did not understand what was said. After a while Ko reported, "Her name is Suna and she is fourteen years old."

"Suna." Shinza repeated the name. "What else did you say to her?"

"Nothing else."

Two days later Shinza went to the farmhouse to find Suna gone. Her wound had healed, but she was in no condition to walk far, so obviously she could not have left by herself.

"Ko!"

Shinza raced back to the village and searched for the house where the Koreans were billeted. He found Ko and spoke to him outside.

"What have you done with the woman?"

"She has gone to Lord Mitsuyoshi."

"What?"

"Lieutenant Kato was looking for women to offer his lordship. The lieutenant and I went to many villages, but we could not find any women. I had no choice but to tell him about Suna."

A black rage rose inside Shinza, a rage so strong that he did not even hear Ko's last words before drawing his sword and killing him on the spot. Leaving the body where it lay, he ran to the house where Lord Mitsuyoshi was staying, his bloodied sword still in his hand. He had lost all control and intended to fight his way into the bedchamber to rescue Suna. However, his way was barred by Kato Zusho, who was a better swordsman in those days. Shinza was thrown to the ground, bound hand and foot, and locked in an empty room.

When the army returned to Japan in 1596, Shinza applied for leave to study the martial arts. He traveled far and wide and did not set foot in his home domain for four years. Only Kato Zusho knew the real reason for this.

"Pimp!" The insult he had flung at Kato Zusho in Korea was rising in his throat again, this time directed at Shinoi Ukyo. The impotent fury he had felt when he failed to rescue the girl from Lord Mitsuyoshi welled up in him once more.

A man carrying a lantern approached and stopped when he saw them.

"Is that you, Saku?"

It was Heishiro. Saku ran to him and buried her head in her brother's chest.

"It's taken you a long time to get here. What have you been doing?" Shinza demanded.

"Making the Mikamis reveal what had happened to Saku took longer than expected. I was just on my way to the castle."

"The castle?" Shinza asked, a malicious glint in his eyes caught by the light of the lantern. "Were you planning to talk with the lord?"

"Yes."

"Well, no matter now. Hand me the lantern. It's difficult for an old man to see at night." Taking it, Shinza began to walk away.

"Where are you going?"

"Need you ask? To Shinoi's residence."

"In that case, let me come with you."

"No, you take Saku home."

Lengthening his stride, Shinza hurried away.

"Be on your guard," Heishiro called out. "Shinoi Ukyo has gathered a lot of fighting men around him."

Shinoi Ukyo's residence was set in a large garden situated by the moat in front of the castle's northern gate. It was about nine o'clock when Shinza arrived. He did not wait for anyone to greet him but strode through the door and down the corridor without pausing. Several people tried to detain him, but one glance at his face convinced them of the futility of this.

Ukyo was in the middle of entertaining seven or eight guests in a room at the rear of the house when Shinza flung open the doors. He recognized two or three high-ranking retainers, but his appearance brought a sudden hush to the party. Ukyo occupied the seat of honor, directly in front of the tokonoma alcove, which was decorated with a hanging scroll and a flower arrangement.

"What are you doing?" demanded Ukyo when he found his voice. "Is there no limit to your insolence?" The alcohol he had consumed combined with his outrage to turn his face a liverish red. Seizing his saké cup, he flung it at Shinza.

Shinza dodged and sat down opposite Ukyo.

"I know exactly what you tried to do with Inukai's daughter."

Panic flitted across Ukyo's face.

"I have no idea what you're talking about."

"You're no better than an animal. The sight of your arrogant face has become so abhorrent to me that I am here to take your life."

"What? Did Kato send you?"

Flinging himself backwards, Ukyo twisted his bloated body around to reach for his sword, which was on a rack in the alcove behind him. Shinza rose smoothly to one knee, drew his sword, and brought the blade down on Ukyo's exposed shoulder in one smooth movement. Ukyo collapsed to the floor with a scream as blood gushed from the wound and spattered on the painting in the alcove with a sound like a bucket of water hitting the ground.

The guests in the room all leaped up and watched as Shinza slowly got to his feet, acting as if nothing was amiss.

"As you see, Ukyo and I had a disagreement and I was forced to kill him," he said calmly. "I have no quarrel with any of you, so if you will excuse me I will leave now."

As he turned toward the door, the guests moved silently out of his way. Once he was in the corridor outside, however, his way was barred by a huge figure holding an unsheathed sword.

"Will you let me pass, please?" Shinza asked, watching him carefully, but the man merely grinned.

As Shinza took a step forward, the man backed nimbly into the adjacent room. Shinza, equally swift, moved forward and forced him into a corner. They were so close that their chests were almost touching, and there was the grating sound of metal on metal as their swordguards clashed. Shinza glared at his opponent, whose forehead was covered in sweat.

Finally, the man tried to slip to one side, but Shinza's sword flashed out as he did so. His opponent twisted to ward off the blow, but the next instant he fell to his knees and collapsed on the floor, blood welling out to form a dark stain on the tatami mats.

"That technique is known as the 'stone-cutter.' It's been a long time since I last used it," Shinza remarked as he sheathed his sword and straightened his clothes. He spoke quietly, but a tense undercurrent in his voice dissuaded anyone else from trying to stop him.

"I do not intend to run or hide, so if anybody is dissatisfied with the evening's events, come to my house. Jibu Shinza will be pleased to meet any challenges."

With that, he turned and walked toward the front door. Nobody blocked his path.

"It shouldn't be taking him so long," muttered Shinza. As a precaution he had watch fires burning inside the garden gate to light up the front of the house and the street outside, but there was no sign of anyone approaching.

"Do you mean Heishiro?" Yoshie asked.

No, he thought irritably, recalling the scene he had witnessed earlier.

He had returned home to find Heishiro waiting for him. This was to be expected, but it was Heishiro's general attitude that Shinza found objectionable. The young man had been exchanging lighthearted chatter with Yoshie when Shinza entered the house, and as he walked through to the living room he could hear the two laughing. They looked up uncomfortably when they saw him and immediately adopted a more formal manner, but he was not pleased. He had just put his life at risk, yet here they were, talking and carrying on without a care in the world.

He glared at them, his expression grim as he recounted the events at Shinoi's residence. He also tried to shock them by saying he was expecting an attack on his house as soon as Shinoi's followers could prepare for it. Yoshie turned pale and looked suitably dismayed.

"I will go and get ready to fight." Heishiro rose to his feet and left the house. His movements were slow, almost casual. Since then they had not heard from him, and the house next door remained quiet.

With Heishiro's departure, Shinza hurriedly made preparations to defend his own house. He had given weapons to Yoshie and his servant, Gohei, and had ordered the latter to light the watch fires in the garden. He did not know whether the Shinoi family would really attack or not, but it was a large family so quite a few of them might respond to a call for revenge. He was expecting them to retaliate, especially after seeing the head of the household cut down before their eyes. On the other hand, they probably realized that if too many of them became involved, the matter would no longer be regarded as a private vendetta and would take on a more serious aspect. They were very likely taking time to select the members to participate in the attack.

Yoshie cut a gallant figure, with the white headband around her forehead and soft leather footwear, the hem of her kimono tucked into her sash, and a short spear in her hand. Old Gohei stood on guard beside the gate, his normally bent back as straight as a ramrod as he peered up and down the street, watching for any sign of attackers. He was also armed with a spear. When Gohei first heard what had happened, the color had drained from his face, but he did not flinch from his duty. He had served the Jibu family for many years and had accompanied Shinza to war on numerous occasions.

However, Shinza knew that if the enemy came in force, there was no chance of repelling them. He could take care of five or six single-handedly, but it would go badly if there were more than that. Yoshie's brave show suddenly seemed rather pathetic.

"By the way," he blurted out, "I've noticed that you seem very close with the boy next door."

Yoshie looked at her father in surprise.

"Is there some kind of understanding between you?" he asked.

She looked at her father's face intently for a few moments, then burst into laughter.

"No, there's nothing like that. There's nothing between us."

Shinza felt disappointed, but Yoshie seemed to be speaking with complete candor so he could only believe her.

"We're just good friends and neighbors," Yoshie said. "If there were more to it than that, it would be most awkward. I know I must marry somebody who can become head of the Jibu family, and Heishiro is the eldest son and the head of the Inukai family. I know what's expected of me, so don't worry."

"That's all right then," was Shinza's gruff response, but he was still not completely satisfied. Surely there was more between them than that. After all, Heishiro was now twenty-five years old and should have found a wife. And Yoshie was eighteen. Although she was confident that she would find a husband easily, nobody knew better than Shinza that a father-in-law as unpopular as he was might make things more difficult than she thought.

Heishiro was the only man in the domain who seemed impervious to his sarcasm, but as head of the Inukai family he was ineligible to be Yoshie's husband.

"A long time ago," Yoshie began hesitantly, "Heishiro joked that he might turn over his role as family head to his brother and marry me."

"He joked?" Shinza said indignantly. "What impertinence! And what did you say?"

"Why are you getting angry? It was only a joke."

Just as I thought, Shinza brooded. He feels an attachment to her but is afraid to tell her directly, so he does it in a roundabout way. It's not manly.

He said to Yoshie, "You should make him more responsible for what he says. Don't let him pass it off as a joke."

"Why are you so cross?"

"He's in love with you."

"Father!" She was so embarrassed at this that she hid her face in her hands, her spear clattering to the ground.

"He's a coward who's afraid to say that straight to your face despite the fact that he's in and out of this house all the time like a mouse or something. You needn't be so shy. Make him stand by what he says. Tell him that if he's in love with you he should act accordingly. He has Saku and his brother, Gennosuke, to carry on the family name."

"It's not Gennosuke. It's Kennosuke," Yoshie said, cheerfully correcting him.

"Anyway, where on earth is he?" Shinza said impatiently. "Is he scared to use his sword? Maybe he's hiding in bed."

"Don't insult him, Father," Yoshie protested. "Heishiro is the acting head of the Tanimoto sword fighting dojo."

It was the first Shinza had heard that. For once he was lost for words.

"Sorry to be so long," Heishiro said as he came through the gate. He was still in the same clothes and was not wearing any armor.

"Why are you not properly dressed?" Shinza demanded, glaring at him.

"There's no more cause for concern," Heishiro said. He had been running and was perspiring heavily. "Everything is settled."

Apparently, Heishiro had left Shinza's house and rushed to Kato Zusho's estate to explain the situation. Zusho had reacted so swiftly that it was as though he had been waiting for something like this. He had summoned Chief Censor Handa Sakubei and ordered him to secure the Shinoi residence. He had then called Naganuma Tarozaemon and Hoshina Rinya, and the three had gone to the castle to confront the daimyo, Nobutaka, in his bedchamber. There they presented him with a letter signed by all of them.

A messenger from the castle had arrived at Kato's estate a short while before to announce that the Shinoi family had been banished from the domain. Their supporters—Chief Councilor Shiino Hikobei, Councilor Yamagata Takizo, and Lieutenant Akamatsu Chuta—had all been confined to their homes.

Shinza responded with no more than a grunt, but he could not deny feeling relieved. He was impressed by his future son-in-law's quick wits—then discomforted that he had caught himself thinking of Heishiro as Yoshie's husband. He shouted to Gohei to close the gate and put out the fires in the braziers.

He presumed that Heishiro would take the hint and go home, for he was not prepared to show him too much friendliness yet. However, when he turned around he saw the two young people standing together.

"The headband suits you, Yoshie. You look even lovelier than usual," Heishiro said.

Shinza clicked his tongue in disgust. Had the boy no shame, talking to her like that in front of her father?

"You must be exhausted. Come in and have some tea before you go home." She was probably just reacting to his compliment, but her voice sounded more alluring than ever. The two turned and entered the house together. Then, realizing that Shinza was still outside, Yoshie turned.

"Father, would you like some tea, too?"

Shinza knew she was only saying this out of politeness.

"Don't worry about me. If I have tea at this time of night I'll never get to sleep." The sarcastic overtone to his excuse was wasted on the couple, however. He stood in the garden listening to their happy laughter, while Gohei put out the fires. From the sound of Yoshie's voice, he understood that she was just as much in love with Heishiro as he was with her.

Gohei came over to Shinza, his face a mass of wrinkles as he grinned.

"They make a good couple, don't they, sir?"

"Humph.!" Shinza scowled, but as Gohei doused the last remaining embers, he could not prevent a happy smile from breaking out on his face.

Out of Luck

The Osan bar in Edo's Ryogoku district was named after its owner, a woman who was famed for her beauty back in the days before the area was developed and the bar was little more than a shack by the river. Now Osan was nearly fifty years old, and on the rare occasions when she came to serve in the bar herself, nobody but longtime regulars gave her a second glance.

Each night a group of young men would congregate in one corner of the bar, and as time passed the members became more or less fixed. Sometimes there was as many as six or seven, at others only three or four, but every evening they were to be found there, huddled together and talking furtively. When other customers came into the bar, they would stare at them insolently, and occasionally burst into raucous laughter or shout to one another, showing little consideration for anyone else.

The owner herself took a dim view of this kind of behavior, and when she felt they had overstepped the mark, she would come over and admonish them. That would usually quiet them down, but if they thought she was being unreasonable, they would protest vociferously, reminding her that they were customers, too.

They liked to show off, but she did not think they were as tough as they made themselves out to be. The tall, pallid youth with an affected manner of speaking was the son of the candle dealer in Yonezawa; the swarthy, well-built youth was the third son of the handyman who lived at the corner of Heiemon. All the others, too, were from the neighborhood and everybody knew their family backgrounds. The young men met at the bar to discuss how to pick up women or, if they had the cash, they would move from the bar to the brothel area across the river. There was also an illegal gambling joint somewhere in the neighborhood, which they would sometimes talk about in hushed voices.

Osan did not like them meeting at her bar every night, but she was prepared to put up with them as long as they did not bother the other customers. She knew that young bloods had a tendency to behave recklessly. At nineteen or twenty years of age they thought they knew it all. They ignored what their parents told them and did as they pleased. She believed that young people knew nothing about life until they were married and had children, but at their age they could not be expected to understand this.

After all, I was just the same, Osan thought, looking over at them indulgently. Just as long as they don't get carried away—always a danger with young men.

In truth, however, the group in the corner was not quite as innocent as she imagined.

"I don't have an endless supply of cash, you know," said Shintaro, the son of the candle dealer. "The other week my old man caught me with my hand in the cash box. He gave me hell! He even threatened to disown me." Shintaro spoke in a feminine way, but his face remained expressionless.

"Hey, nobody's expecting you to pay for us," replied a youth with a flattish face and a protruding lower lip. "The least we can do is pay for our own women."

"It's strange, isn't it? We always manage to find the cash to go gambling." This was from the handyman's son. "If only I could have another big win at dice, like the last time when I treated you all to women in Tokiwa!"

Tonight there were five of them in the bar, and as the speaker looked at each of them in turn, he was pleased to see them nodding agreement. Then, scratching his head, he added, "The trouble is that it only happens once a year. If it weren't for Shintaro, I wouldn't be able to afford a woman most of the time."

"Have you got the guts to break into my house?" Shintaro asked out of the blue. The fact that he could propose something so bizarre without any change of expression revealed how outrageous he could be. "I can't help you do it, but if Nao and Yoshizo are game, I can tell you where the money is."

"You must be kidding," Yoshizo replied with an ingratiating laugh. He was the one with the flattish face. "You know, I think Shintaro must be the biggest villain of us all."

"How about you, then?" Shintaro asked, turning towards the other two with a wicked grin. "Do you feel like giving it a go?" One of them laughed noncommittally; the other said it was not worth the risk. This was Sanjiro, a good-looking man despite his narrow, sloping shoulders.

"Unlike Nao and Yoshizo, I don't have any trouble finding women," Sanjiro scoffed. "I've got women chasing after me offering me money, so I don't need to break into anyone's house to get cash for a good time."

"That's probably so," was Yoshizo's shrill response. "That's why you've got a reputation as a playboy." Then he leaned forward and lowered his voice. "What about the girl who was here the other week? The one you caught sight of and followed out—you know, the plump one."

"Oh, I had her," replied Sanjiro, arrogantly thrusting out his chest and smirking. "I took her out for a drink and then we went somewhere we could be alone. She was a virgin, just as I thought. She wasn't much to look at, but she had a great figure."

"Damn it. I wish it had been me," the handyman's son said enviously. "Are you still seeing her?"

"No. Afterwards she told me that she's the only daughter of some rice merchant. Daughters who are only children are nothing but trouble, so once was enough for me."

"What a waste!"

"All of you had better watch out, too," Sanjiro warned. "Only daughters are pampered from the day they're born. They don't have a clue about the real world. One time I had one who kept pestering me to meet her parents. I had a terrible time getting rid of her."

Sanjiro was so busy imparting the fruits of his wisdom about women to his friends that he did not notice someone entering the bar—a huge bear of a man about fifty years of age.

The man paused in the doorway a moment and looked around the bar. Seeing the young men sitting in one corner, he strode over to them. He was dressed like a merchant, but the thick stubble on his cheeks gave him a rather disreputable air.

"Which one of you is Sanjiro?" His voice was loud and resonant, as one would expect from such a large man. The five looked up at him without saying anything, taken aback by his size.

"That's me. And who wants to know?" Sanjiro replied finally, with an attempt at bluster.

"I'm Otsugi's father," the burly giant replied with a grin. His eyes, his nose, and his mouth were all big, and the overall impression he conveyed was anything but friendly. When he laughed, the effect was quite terrifying.

The others looked at Sanjiro, who had turned pale.

"If you're Sanjiro, we have a lot of talking to do. Come with me. My daughter's waiting outside."

"I don't know anyone named Otsugi," Sanjiro replied, his face becoming even whiter. "I think you must have the wrong person, mister."

"Just call me Dad," the man said, grinning again, his eyes shrinking to narrow slits. "There is nothing to be embarrassed about. What you did is perfectly normal for young people. When I got married, Otsugi was already in my old woman's belly. Had the wedding just in time! Ha-ha-ha!" He seemed to find this very amusing, but nobody else was laughing. "My daughter told me all about you. I hear you took quite a fancy to her. It's funny, isn't it? You never know what fate has in store for you."

Sanjiro did not utter a word.

"Anyway, she's our only child. I've spent years looking for the right husband for her, but I couldn't find anyone suitable. Now I can rest easy at last."

"Husband?"

"That's right. Anyway, I want you to come with me to the house. I hear you're a craftsman of some kind, so we need to discuss how you'll give that up and other such matters."

"I'm not going!" Sanjiro moved back, but his retreat was blocked by the wall. There was no escape that way. "You must be joking. I'm only twenty-two! There's no way I want to become the son of a rice merchant."

"What's wrong with it, Sanjiro? I'm sure you'll make a lovely rice merchant," cooed Shintaro, affecting a womanly softness and making the others burst out laughing. They had heard enough to understand the situation. The giant standing in front of them was the father of the girl Sanjiro had just boasted about having seduced. This time the notorious playboy had clearly chosen the wrong girl.

Sanjiro's friends could not imagine him agreeing to marry the girl and settling down as a rice merchant. Just thinking of how he was wracking his brains to get out of this predicament was enough to make them dissolve into laughter.

The big man did not find it at all amusing, though. He stared at Sanjiro coldly.

"You think I'm joking?" He took a step toward him. "You little punk," he said, his tone turning menacing. "Are you telling me that you seduced my precious little girl as a joke?"

"Now calm down," began Naokichi, the handyman's son, planting himself between the two. He was a muscular youth with broad shoulders, but he was dwarfed by the rice merchant. Despite this, he stood with arms akimbo and said, "'Joke' was an unfortunate choice of word, mister. It's just so sudden that it's come as a shock to Sanjiro. What we need to do is . . ."

"I'm not talking to you." The big man swept him aside with one arm as though he were brushing off a fly. His arm was dark and gnarled, like the branch of an old pine tree, and it sent Naokichi flying headfirst into the wall. The other young men were rooted to their seats. He took another step forward. Sanjiro tried to slip out under his arm, but the man was too quick and caught him by the sash around his waist.

"Anyway," he said, resuming his relaxed manner, "you'd better come on over to my house. We can't talk here."

"What's all this ruckus?" asked Osan, coming out of the back room. There were only two or three other customers sitting at one end of the counter, but when Sanjiro tried to escape he had sent a stool flying and the noise had brought her out to investigate.

"Why, if it isn't Osan, the beauty of Yagenbori," the man said, turning around. "I didn't know you were still working."

"I thought I saw a big man come in, but I never dreamed it was you, Riemon."

She was flattered at being called a beauty after all these years, and her voice took on a silky softness. Then, seeing Sanjiro being held by his sash, she frowned. "Has the youngster done something to annoy you?"

"No, nothing like that," the man replied good-naturedly. "I just have a few things to discuss with him. Only nice things, so don't you worry."

"I hope that's true," she said, sounding worried despite his tone. "But no violence. Please don't resort to violence."

"You always were a worrier. I'm a changed man now. My wife nags me, my daughter nags me, and I just do as I'm told," Riemon said with a guffaw. Then, with a wave to Osan, he hauled Sanjiro to his feet and marched him out of the bar.

Once in the street, he released Sanjiro's sash and grasped him by his wrist instead. They walked a short way through the gathering darkness until they came to a young woman standing by the road. Her face was a little on the plump side, but she had a good figure. At their approach she looked up and broke into a smile.

"Sanjiro," she called out happily. Sanjiro glanced at her, then looked away.

"Go away," he muttered, but her father increased the pressure on his wrist until he thought it would break. "Otsugi, thank you for coming to meet me," he said aloud.

"Here, take a look at this," said Sanjiro, slipping an arm out of his kimono to show Yoshizo his shoulder. His skin was as soft and white as a woman's, but his shoulder was disfigured by an ugly, painful-looking swelling. He tucked his arm back in.

"I have to carry these rice bales into the storehouse behind the shop. Each of them weighs a hundred and twenty pounds. Then I have to take them from the storehouse into the shop. Every evening a cart brings another load of bales. I have to do this every day while her old man looks on with a thick bamboo stick in his hand."

"That's terrible," said Yoshizo sympathetically. He had inherited his father's trade, crafting containers from thin strips of cypress wood, and he lived with his mother so he did not need to spend much and life was easy. The two were sitting in his workshop. Yoshizo had no apprentices so there was no fear of being overheard. "It must be hard work carting all that rice around, but you don't do it all day, do you? Surely you get to sit in the store when it's open, so you can rest then."

"You're joking," Sanjiro said. Exposing his leg, he said, "Look at that! It's swollen, right?"

"Let's see," Yoshizo said, bending down to examine the leg. "It doesn't look swollen to me."

"Well, it is. It's all puffy."

Sanjiro went on to explain that next to the store there was a shed with a huge mortar-and-pestle contraption for polishing rice. It was operated by a treadle, and it was his job to work this all day.

"I'm not even allowed into the store. I'm nothing but a slave! A slave, I tell you! And her father keeps coming over with his stick to make sure I don't stop working. My whole body's falling apart. I'd have died if I'd stayed any longer, so when I saw a chance to escape I took it."

In his younger days, Sanjiro had been apprenticed to a man who made writing brushes, but he had been dismissed for repeatedly breaking the rules. He had no family or relatives, so thereafter he had worked for a succession of brushmakers, earning just enough to survive and leaving as soon as he became bored. He was the living image of a wastrel, and although he had a deft hand when it came to women, he had never had to lift anything heavier than the brushes he made.

"It sounds really tough," Yoshizo said, looking closely at his friend's face. "But at night you get to sleep with the girl—what's her name?—Otsugi. That must count for something."

"Sleep with her?" Sanjiro shook his hand. "She won't even talk to me! I hardly ever see her. I think her father must have told her to keep away from me."

Yoshizo burst out laughing.

"So they're just making you work without pay? You poor fool! Who'd have thought it? Playboy Sanjiro going without a woman and spending his time polishing rice."

"Not that I want a woman like her around," Sanjiro said, momentarily slipping back into his old playboy role. Then, looking woebegone again, he said, "I think she's in it with her father. I told you they treat me like a slave. Well, he's such a tyrant he can't get anybody to work for him for long. I think they tricked me into sleeping with her just to get me to do their manual labor for them."

"In that case you should have run away sooner. Surely you're not going to tell me that you're being guarded all night."

"I can't get out. Come bedtime, he locks all the doors himself and checks the entire house. I tried climbing over the fence recently. But I fell down and he heard the noise and gave me a real thrashing with that bamboo stick of his. I've still got the scars to prove it. Look!" He turned around and lifted his clothing to reveal purple bruises covering his backside.

"That's terrible! I'm surprised you've managed to put up with it as long as you have," Yoshizo said.

"That's why I want you to let me stay here, just for two or three days."

"No problem. He sounds a real bully. Just let him come here looking for you and I'll soon get rid of him."

"Thanks. You're a real friend."

"Stay as long as you like. But you can't spend the rest of your life hiding. What are you going to do?"

"I thought I'd go over to the Otowa district. I used to work with somebody there and I'm going to ask him to help me. Her father will never think of looking for me there."

Just then Yoshizo's mother called to him from the house, saying he had a visitor.

"I'll be back in a minute," Yoshizo said, slipping out of the workshop only to return almost immediately, his face ashen. Following on his heels was none other than Riemon, the rice merchant.

"Oh, there you are," Riemon said, with a happy laugh. "When we found you'd left home, Otsugi burst into tears, my wife lost her temper, and the whole house was in uproar."

Sanjiro stood up and looked around desperately, but the workshop had only two small windows. There was no way out except through the door, which was blocked by Riemon. Dazed, Sanjiro sat down again, but Riemon stretched out a huge hand and beckoned him with his finger.

"I went to that bar to ask Osan where your friends lived and then started visiting them one by one. Luckily, this is only the third house I've been to."

Yoshizo stood and watched as the rice merchant bid his mother a cheerful farewell and led Sanjiro out. The next moment he heard the sound of running feet outside the window and, looking out, he saw Sanjiro making a dash for freedom with Riemon panting in pursuit. The escape did not last long, however, for Riemon caught up with him outside the fish seller's shop on the other side of the street, gripped him firmly by the wrist, and led him away.

Two years passed. One day Yoshizo was walking through Mishima in Kanda when he spotted Sanjiro unloading rice bales from a cart. Yoshizo could hardly believe his eyes. Sanjiro was tossing them effortlessly onto his shoulder and carrying them inside the store with a sure step. The carter and the store servant were working alongside him, and Sanjiro was hefting the bales with an ease equal to theirs. He piled up twenty bales without a break, then walked to the shed behind the store.

Cutting open a bale, Sanjiro lifted it up easily and poured the rice, still with the husks on, into the large stone mortar. Then he began working the heavy treadle to polish the rice. There was little light in the shed, and the monotonous thump-thump of the pestle was soporific, but Sanjiro continued doggedly.

A shadow fell across the doorway, and a young woman called out Sanjiro's name. It was Otsugi.

"What is it?" Sanjiro demanded, without pausing in his work.

"Nothing really."

"In that case, go away. Can't you see I'm busy?" he said shortly. Otsugi ignored him and entered the shed.

"That looks like hard work."

"It is. Luckily I'm so tired at the end of the day that I have no energy to think about women."

"Don't you even think about me?"

"Never."

Otsugi ignored Sanjiro's rudeness and moved closer.

"Father says you'll make a good rice merchant. Soon he's going to let you work in the store. He wants you to learn how to do the books and sit at the counter."

"A good rice merchant? Ha!"

He vented his anger by stomping harder on the treadle. The noise in the shed became deafening.

"Careful! The rice will spill out," Otsugi warned, but he paid her no attention.

"I never wanted to be a rice merchant. You and your father tricked me into working for you as a slave."

"You've got it all wrong," Otsugi replied. "Father said he was going to turn you into a first-rate merchant and he didn't want me hanging around you and getting in the way. I just did what I was told. I never tricked you. What a horrible thing to say!"

"What do you want me to say? It's not so bad now that I'm used to the work, but in the beginning my shoulder was bruised and swollen, my body was a mass of aches and pains, and I thought I was going to die. Do you expect me to thank you for allowing me to work for free all this time?"

"I know it's been hard on you. Sometimes I couldn't help crying when I saw the state you were in."

"That's easy to say."

"Father believed he was doing what was best for you. Looking at you now, I can see he was right. You're twice the man you used to be."

"Don't give me that," Sanjiro said, stopping the treadle and looking at her. "I know why your father's doing this. I'm the man who slept with his precious daughter, so he wants to work me to the bone and make an example of me in case anybody else might be tempted. He's doing what's best for me? Don't make me laugh! I'm no fool, you know. I realized what was going on, but I couldn't do anything about it. Your father's stronger than me, so I just buckled under and did as I was told. But give me time and I'll get my revenge."

"Do you still think that way?"

"Of course!" Sanjiro shouted. "He may be bigger than me, but he's getting older. One of these days I'll pay him back for what he's done and be out of here."

"Oh," Otsugi muttered dejectedly, her shoulders drooping and the spark fading from her eyes. "If that's how you feel, there's no need to wait," she continued, without looking at him. "You can go now. I'll explain things to Father."

"Hey, just a moment!" Sanjiro said, but Otsugi had already turned and was making for the door. Sanjiro jumped down from the treadle and hurried after her, catching her by the shoulders as she was leaving the shed. "Wait!"

"Let go of me," she replied, trying to wriggle out of his grasp.

"You haven't got anything to say to me. After all, you never even liked me."

"That's . . . Well . . ." Sanjiro did not know what to do. The moment she told him he was free to go, he realized that the idea of returning to his carefree ways no longer appealed to him. Compared to the last two years, his former life seemed a shallow existence, hardly what he could call a life at all. If he were to throw everything away now, what was the point of the last two years? He felt this was a job that could give a man real satisfaction, unlike the time when he worked only if he needed money and quit to go looking for women the moment he became bored.

"It would be a waste," Sanjiro said.

Otsugi stopped struggling to free herself and looked up at him, her full red lips just inches from his face. Her looks were no more than average, and there was no way she could change that, but in the last two years she had matured as a woman. Her skin had taken on a creamy whiteness and her figure had filled out.

"It would be a waste to throw away a fine woman like you." He slipped his arm around her waist and pulled her closer, talking like a playboy once again. He had not been near a woman for two years, and he felt a sudden surge of passion. Whisking her lightly off her feet, he carried her to the pile of empty rice bales in a corner of the shed.

"I don't have an endless supply of cash, you know. You have to figure out a way to get some yourself," Shintaro, the candle dealer's son, was saying as a figure appeared in the doorway of the Osan bar and walked over to the corner where they were sitting.

"Hello, stranger," exclaimed Naokichi, the handyman's son, in his high-pitched voice.

"Hey, it's Sanjiro! What a surprise!"

"So you finally managed to escape."

This last comment was from Yoshizo, but, examining his friend more closely, he realized that this was wide of the mark. Sanjiro was wearing an immaculate kimono with a subdued striped pattern, and he was carrying a parcel neatly wrapped in a piece of cloth. His hair was in a smart topknot, and he seemed fitter than he had ever been. In fact, he looked every inch the successful young merchant.

"It appears you've settled in with the rice merchant."

"Yes," Sanjiro replied with an embarrassed laugh as he looked at his old friends. "Our first child is coming soon. I had some business over here, so I thought I'd drop in to see how you're all doing."

"So even playboy Sanjiro's luck ran out in the end," Naokichi said.

"Yes, I guess you could say that I'm finally out of luck," Sanjiro responded. His former friends seemed seedier than he remembered. He hesitated a moment, then looked toward the bar counter and ordered a cup of tea.

The Runaway Stallion

The mansion belonging to Vice Councilor Usui Kuranosuke was such a huge, sprawling building that any conversation held in the rear drawing room could not possibly be heard from the street.

Even so, this evening Usui and his guest were sitting close together, speaking in whispers by the light of a single lamp. The visitor was Moriya Ichinoshin, a pale-faced official from the treasury. He was a little over thirty years of age and gave the impression of being rather superficial, but in fact he was a shrewd man holding a position of some responsibility.

"You're certain those are Shingu's actual words?" Usui asked. His voice was low, but the intensity of his gaze made it clear that he was shaken by the news Moriya Ichinoshin had brought him.

"Yes, absolutely," Ichinoshin replied earnestly.

Usui's eyes were fixed on the younger man's tense face as he spoke. Then he sat up straighter and folded his arms. Usui was forty-two years old. He was wearing a cool summer kimono of white linen, and in both appearance and build he looked every inch a figure of authority.

"I don't like it," said Usui, turning his gaze to the shrubs in the garden, barely visible in the lamplight. "I don't like the fact that Mitani informed him in advance."

"I agree," Ichinoshin responded, and Usui's eyes swung back to his face.

Usui Kuranosuke was the most powerful man in the domain. Although Chief Councilor Sugimori Shobei was nominally in charge, he was too old to come to the castle regularly and was considered a mere figurehead. The daimyo, Shigeoki, was sick and bedridden in Edo, and for several years had been unable to return to his home province, leaving the young Vice Councilor Usui with virtually a free hand in domain politics.

That Usui possessed such power was a fact known only to a handful of people. Usui had enlisted the aid of a wealthy merchant by the name of Shinkaiya and had used his money to develop new industries in the domain, such as sericulture and forestry. He also had canals dug and roads built to promote farming in the more remote regions, and had arranged cheap loans to poorer samurai retainers. As a result, he was regarded by most as an extremely gifted administrator.

By cooperating with Usui, Shinkaiya had lent the domain vast sums of money that could never be repaid, and as he grew rich from the interest on the loans, he also received numerous privileges that helped him expand his business. In return, he paid a handsome bribe to Usui every year, which enabled the latter to keep mistresses in town and live far beyond his means—all of course concealed behind a façade of respectability.

Two years earlier, however, Usui began to suspect that Chamberlain Mitani Jinjuro, who was assigned to the capital in Edo, had somehow discovered the relationship between the merchant and himself. Last year and the year before Mitani had held secret talks with Shinkaiya's main rival, another merchant of substance called Tokuraya, on his return to the castle town on official visits.

The news that Ichinoshin had brought tonight seemed to confirm Usui's worst suspicions. Mitani had sent a messenger with a personal letter from the daimyo to Councilor Shingu Kozaemon. Ichinoshin was a spy that Usui had managed to insinuate into Shingu's inner circle.

Councilor Shingu was forty years old, two years younger than Usui, and had only been promoted to his post two years earlier. He had made no attempt to form a clique against Usui, but as he was the scion of a noble family, people naturally gravitated toward him. Usui believed that eventually Shingu would gather a powerful faction against him, which was why he had Ichinoshin worm his way into Shingu's confidence. His foresight had paid off, and nobody suspected that Ichinoshin was working for him.

"So what should we do?" Usui asked. He unfolded his arms and rubbed his chin with one hand, stealing a glance at Ichinoshin. "It would be most unfortunate if the daimyo's letter were to reach Shingu, but it would be an act of treason to seize it by force."

"We should take it," Ichinoshin said. "Mitani has arranged for the daimyo to write a letter from his sickbed, to be sent not to you but to Shingu. The letter is secret. It might cause trouble if it were delivered."

"It might cause more trouble if it were not," Usui replied. "Depending on the contents, Mitani might be able to deduce who's responsible."

"If there's no proof, we can bluff our way through. The way matters stand, it's more dangerous for us to ignore the letter than to steal it."

Usui looked up in surprise, realizing that Ichinoshin's assessment was correct. The first thing he had to discover was whether the letter concerned him or not. If it did relate to his secret deals he could take some action, but he was powerless to act as long as he did not know what was in the letter. Ichinoshin had gone straight to the heart of the matter. Usui had been judging his accomplice only from outward appearances; he had forgotten how cunning he could be.

"When is the messenger due?"

"In five days, on August the second. He is expected to reach the Fujikake border post in the early evening."

"That means he won't get into town until ten or eleven at night. As long as we know that, it will be easy to make the necessary arrangements."

"There is one problem, though," Ichinoshin said. "The messenger is Taguchi Shozo, one of the daimyo's personal attendants, and Mitani has ordered an escort to accompany him from the border into town."

"An escort?" Usui felt his suspicions increase. If Mitani had ordered an escort, he must be expecting an attack on the messenger. And who else would be likely to do that other than himself? In that case, he had no alternative but to assume the worst and fight back.

"Is the escort to be large?"

"No." Ichinoshin smiled. "Mitani told us to choose one capable man in order to avoid attracting attention. Actually, I was summoned this evening and told to suggest someone suitable."

"You certainly do seem to have won his trust." Usui gave a cheerful laugh. For the present, he was still in control of the situation. "We should have no difficulty then. Just make sure it's a swordsman who's not too strong, yet not so weak as to arouse suspicion."

Even as he said this, one name sprang to his mind. In his younger days, Usui had had a rival both in sword fighting and in love, a man who had caused him much bitterness but who was now down on his luck and held the lowly position of chief groom. That man had lost his wife ten years earlier and had never remarried, preferring to drown his sorrow in drink. As Usui visualized this miserable figure, his features contorted into a vicious sneer.

"Any idea who you'll choose?"

"Not yet."

"In that case there's somebody I'd like to recommend. He's ideal for the task."

"Who's that?"

"Have you ever heard of someone called Tsubuki Jubei?"

"Let me think."

"You probably haven't. He used to be one of the daimyo's personal guards until he committed a blunder and was demoted to the stables. He's the same age as me and is an expert in the Mugai style of sword fighting. If you mention his name to Shingu, I'm sure he will agree."

For ten years now there had been little mention of Tsubuki Jubei's exploits with the sword. Better known was the fact that he could be found drinking every night in the back streets of Hatsune. Usui knew that he was no longer the man he used to be and that, despite his reputation as a swordsman, he had become a middle-aged alcoholic who could not be bothered to keep fit. Usui could think of nobody better suited to his purposes, although he was unnerved by the degree of animosity he still felt toward the man.

"We don't want anybody who's too skilled with the sword."

"No need for concern." Usui explained enthusiastically why Jubei was just the man for the job.

His hatred of Jubei had altered strangely over the years, and it now manifested itself in a perverse desire to torment his weakened rival. He wanted Jubei to suffer more. Nothing would give him greater pleasure.

"You might make inquiries, but I think you'll find the situation as I described. Shingu is probably not aware of the man's decline, so I'm sure he will agree with the choice."

After Ichinoshin left, Usui remained sitting with his arms folded. Now that he was alone, he could hear the insects chirping in the garden. As the sound crescendoed, his uneasiness grew. Ichinoshin had said that all they had to do was steal the letter, but he no longer believed that would be sufficient. He could not rid himself of the feeling that he was being backed into a corner, and he wondered what Mitani had discovered.

The more he thought about it, the angrier he became.

Who do they think they are? he thought in disgust. If I had not made Shinkaiya put up his money, the rivers would have burst their banks, the clan would not have been able to afford the daimyo's journeys to Edo, and the farmers, who were reduced to eating millet gruel and salt during the last famine, would never have recovered. If they are accusing me of something, they should do so to my face.

However, once his rage was spent, he had to admit that he had occasionally allowed himself to go too far. That was what worried him, but there was no turning back now.

He walked out onto the veranda and called for some tea. He knew that he would not be able to sleep for some time that night.

As Usui was ordering tea, Ichinoshin finally emerged from the shadows beneath the gate, where he had been hiding to make sure nobody was around. As an extra precaution, he took a strip of cloth from inside his kimono and wrapped it around the lower part of his face before setting out. The day had been fine and the road still retained the sun's heat, but the sky was now overcast and Ichinoshin soon vanished into the darkness.

The Shirozumiya tavern was located in a back street of Hatsune. The interior was divided into two: the section along the wall with a raised floor was reserved for samurai, while the earthen-floored area in front of the kitchen, taking up most of the space, had tables where the lower classes could eat and drink. Naturally, some people objected to rules of any sort, and occasionally a samurai would sit among the townsmen, glaring around himself as if to challenge anyone who may wish to complain.

Tsubuki Jubei was not such a samurai. He was sitting in the area set aside for townsfolk, but this was only because the tavern was crowded that night and the section for samurai was full. Despite the numerous restaurants and drinking houses in the district, Jubei always claimed that the Shirozumiya served the best saké, so he had no intention of going elsewhere. The tavern was dimly lit and rather dirty, with not particularly good food, but the saké was excellent. Jubei liked to sit in a corner by himself and drink—cold saké in summer and hot saké in winter—to dispel his gloomy thoughts.

Tonight he was enjoying his drink, happy to have found a seat. He ordered some grilled mackerel and yam stew. Just as he was beginning to feel the customary euphoric effects of the alcohol, a shadow fell over his mood, and he realized the reason was Moto.

He was not proud of his nightly excursions to the tavern and would try to slip out of the house unnoticed, but no matter where she might be Moto always heard him and rushed to the door to see him off. She was always cheerful and would urge him in a loud voice to be careful on his way home. Tonight had been different.

"Are you going to Hatsune again?" There was a sadness in her voice.

Adding that she had something she wished to discuss with him, she asked him to come home early and not to drink too much.

What can she want to talk about? Jubei wondered.

Moto was a member of the Aiba family and a distant relative who had come to live in his house and assist with the housework. When Jubei's wife had died, he was left with a daughter to raise and only a cook to help, so his extended family had discussed the situation and decided that Moto should move in with him. That had been five years ago, and she was now thirty-seven years old.

Fair in complexion and with a quiet disposition, Moto had lost her husband two years before Jubei's wife had died, and being childless she had been sent back to live with her parents. When she moved in with Jubei, the family thought the two might make a good couple and eventually marry, but the spark for that kind of relationship was apparently lacking. Despite living in the same house for five years now, they had not grown any closer.

Not that the spark was entirely absent, Jubei thought, pouring himself more saké. One night about a year after Moto moved in, she had come out of the front door to welcome him home from the tavern and he had taken her in his arms quite naturally. However, she had immediately pushed him away.

"You stink of horses!" she had said.

What's wrong with the smell of horses? he had thought, but he did not voice the protest aloud. Her rejection had been enough to kill his interest.

Moto's family was superior to him in rank, with an annual stipend of 1,500 bushels of rice, whereas his income had been decreased from 500 bushels to 325. He was now in charge of the grooms and stableboys, which required him to be at the stables every day. Moreover, he was personally responsible for grooming the horses belonging to the daimyo and his immediate family.

Despite their higher rank, Moto's family had been moved by pity to ask Moto to help Jubei out. Her brother, who was head of the Aiba household, had intimated this when he visited Jubei at the stables one day. Although Jubei realized he needed someone, he objected to the man's condescending manner. He was tempted to protest that it was he who should be thanked for taking a widow off their hands, but in truth Moto was invaluable, and he did not know what he would do without her.

His reaction to her comment about smelling of horses largely resulted from the antagonism he felt toward her family and his disappointment at discovering that she had the same prejudices as them. Ever since that day he had made it a point never to touch her again.

However, this was not the only reason he kept his distance. Once, when Moto was out, Kumé, the old cook, had come to him.

"Master," she said, "I know you must be lonely, but you must never try to force yourself on Moto."

Jubei was tempted to laugh at Kumé's frank warning, but when he heard the reason he realized she was giving it for his own good.

Kumé told him that one day she had gone to the storehouse to fetch the millstones kept there. It was a glorious late autumn day, with clear blue skies and a warm sun. Nevertheless, Kumé had decided it was a good time to grind some grain in preparation for the coming winter. The two millstones were looped together with rope and were very heavy, but Kumé thought she could manage to drag them out of the storehouse, untie the rope, and carry them into the kitchen one at a time. However, no matter how hard she tried, she could not budge them.

Moto was on the veranda combing her hair at the time. Catching sight of Kumé's futile efforts, she slipped on her sandals and walked over. Holding her hair up at the nape of her neck with one hand, she lifted both milestones in the other and carried them effortlessly to the veranda. Seeing Kumé's look of amazement, she blushed and asked Kumé not to tell Jubei and to keep the incident a secret.

Jubei was stunned. He knew the millstones were heavy even for most men and, if Kumé was not exaggerating, Moto's strength must be truly astounding. She was a woman of few words, but perhaps some unfortunate event in her past had led her to ask Kumé not to mention the incident. It might also explain why she had been sent back to her parents after her husband's death. Whatever the significance, Kumé's story imbued Moto with a certain air of mystery.

The incident itself did not make him avoid Moto, but he had to admit that it did make her less approachable. In time he realized that it was possible to live in the same house with a woman without becoming emotionally involved, and so the situation had continued for five years.

The yams Jubei had ordered had been simmered in soy sauce and dried bonito flakes. They tasted delicious, but as he sat there eating his mood turned darker. Perhaps he should have tried to be closer to Moto. Never laying a finger on her might have been a mistake. She had probably expected more from him and had now made up her mind to leave. The saké suddenly tasted sour. How would he and his daughter, Fusae, get by without her? Who would look after Fusae?

"I'm sorry to interrupt—"

His reverie was broken, and he looked up to see a smartly dressed young man he did not know standing by his table. He did not look like a regular patron of the Shirozumiya.

"Are you Tsubuki Jubei?"

He spoke courteously, and Jubei reluctantly put down his saké cup.

"Yes, I am. And who are you?"

"My name is Moriya Ichinoshin." The man lowered his voice and looked around as if to make sure he was not overheard. The only Moriya whom Jubei could think of was one who lived in Sumiyoshi. He had never seen this man before but guessed it must be his son. He recalled that the Moriyas had a stipend of 750 bushels of rice a year, and he was thinking about this when the man smiled and added, "You probably don't know me. I work for the treasury."

"How can I help you?"

"I would like to discuss a rather sensitive issue. Could you come with me? It will not take long."

"You can talk here," Jubei replied brusquely.

The man's smile possessed a worldliness beyond his years, but to Jubei it appeared forced. Drinking with gloomy people was not to his liking, but neither was drinking with vacuous types like this man.

By now the Shirozumiya's customers, both samurai and townsmen, were all well into their cups and were talking and laughing loudly. None had the slightest interest in what anyone else was saying. The saké was good, and Jubei had no intention of leaving the tavern just yet.

"Yes, but what I have to say is rather secret and concerns clan business."

"Clan business?"

"I understand that you are an expert in the Mugai style of sword fighting," Ichinoshin whispered.

Jubei was taken aback at the compliment. It may have been an exaggeration, but at the same time he felt the stirrings of a pride he thought he had forgotten.

He looked more closely at the man who had reminded him of his past prowess. Then, with feigned offhandedness, he said, "That was a long time ago."

"That is not what the councilor said."

"Which councilor?"

"Councilor Shingu. I have come on his orders. He needs your help." Ichinoshin then proceeded to try to persuade Jubei to accompany him. Otherwise, he said, he would have failed in his mission.

"Well, if the councilor insists," Jubei replied gravely, "who am I to refuse?"

"I am glad you see it that way."

"So where do you want to take me?"

"There's a room booked at the Akebono inn nearby."

Jubei remembered that he had promised to go home early and realized there was little chance of that now. However, in a way he was glad of the excuse to postpone his talk with Moto.

It was almost eleven miles from the castle town to the Fujikake border post, which meant that Jubei had to walk twenty-two miles there and back. Although he had rested a while at the border, by the time he found himself close enough to the town to see its lights, he felt too tired to move another inch.

His feet hurt, and the blisters he had developed had burst, causing flashes of pain to shoot through his legs at every step. The muscles in his thighs ached, and the fat around his stomach that had accumulated over many years of intemperance felt like a dead weight.

I shouldn't drink so much, he thought, panting. He was beginning to regret having accepted the duty of escorting Taguchi Shozo. The previous night both Councilor Shingu and Ichinoshin had assured him that his presence was merely a precaution and there was little likelihood of having to use his sword.

In spite of this, having accepted the task, he intended to drive off any potential attacker. This was not because the councilor's flattery had gone to his head but because he was confident that he could do so. He may be a little rusty, but given his experience he was sure he could defeat the younger samurai in the clan. However, that had been the previous night. Now, having walked twenty-two miles, both his confidence and his pride had evaporated. As he approached the castle town, it was all he could do to keep up with Taguchi Shozo.

It's hard to tell who's escorting whom, Jubei thought self-deprecatingly. If a young townsman were to attack them now with just a stick, he was doubtful whether he could fend him off. With his painful blisters, he was having a hard time just walking.

Despite these dismal thoughts, the lights of the town gradually grew closer and more distinct as they approached the bridge that marked its outer edge. The eighteen-foot-wide Naema River separated the town from the surrounding countryside, and once across it the long journey would be over.

"Taguchi!" he called to the young samurai walking ahead of him. "Let's rest at the bridge ahead."

Taguchi did not reply.

"I know I shouldn't delay you, but my blisters are killing me."

"Blisters?" Taguchi repeated, sounding vexed but slowing down. "Can't you last until we get into town?"

Even as Taguchi spoke, Jubei felt engulfed in a gust of warm, fetid air. Could it be the smell of the samurai who had been lying in wait for them? They were now rushing up out of the rice fields on either sides of the road to block the way, indistinct except as dark shadows in the night.

"It's an ambush! Run!" Jubei bellowed, drawing his sword.

A sword blade whistled nearby, but Jubei easily knocked it aside with his own. His fighting instincts were now aroused, banishing all thought of his blisters or the heaviness of his body.

Swords came at him from three directions. He parried them skillfully, wounding one attacker in the shoulder. However, his body would not move as quickly as it used to. Jubei found himself on the defensive again and received a shallow cut on his forearm.

At that moment a hideous scream came from where Taguchi was fighting. Somebody must have received a fatal blow.

"Taguchi! Taguchi!" Jubei tried to go to his aid, but was stopped by another swordsman's attack, this time receiving a cut in the left thigh a little above the knee. Instinctively he knew it was a bad wound, and with this realization came a strange fatigue. His body suddenly felt as heavy as stone, and his arms and legs lost all coordination. He blocked another blow and struck back, but the weight of his own sword nearly threw him off balance.

This is not good, he thought, aware that unless he did something soon he was going to die right there on the road. With a loud yell, he lashed out at his opponents and then ran down into the rice fields. His heart was racing, his mouth was dry, and his breathing was labored. For a moment he considered lying down and giving up, but he forced himself to run toward where the night was darkest. He raced along the narrow footpath between the fields until he spotted a deep irrigation ditch and threw himself in.

It was not a moment too soon. He had hardly hit the ground when his pursuers charged along the path above him. The ditch was dry and tall grasses on either bank formed a natural roof over him as he lay face up, his sword still drawn, listening for the attackers. His throat remained parched, but his pounding heart gradually slowed.

I wonder how Taguchi managed, he thought, praying that the death-cry he had heard had not been Taguchi's. However, as there had been at least five attackers, even if the younger man were not dead he would have been injured and the secret letter stolen. Once more Jubei regretted having accepted the role of escort. He had failed completely. He should have refused in favor of a younger man, but he had been so confident. He had thought that if he helped the councilor, he might receive a promotion and an increase in income. He cursed his greed.

Suddenly he heard voices approaching and tightened his grip on his sword. His pursuers were returning, this time speaking in normal voices.

"I never thought he could run so fast!"

"He must have given up sword fighting for running."

All three voices sounded young, and the men were laughing as they spoke. They're ridiculing me, Jubei thought.

The men jumped across the ditch where he was hiding and headed back to the riverbank where the attack had taken place. There seemed to be a path leading that way.

"They say that genius grown old is worse than mediocre, and now I know how true that is. When I heard that it had been arranged for Tsubuki Jubei to be the escort, I was a little worried, but he wasn't up to much, just as they promised."

"Yes, it all went well."

"But we were told to finish him off. What will they say when they hear he got away?"

"Things don't always go according to plan. Anyway, it doesn't make much difference if he got away."

Their voices faded as the men reached the road. Jubei heard them calling to their companions there.

Arranged for me? Jubei wondered what this meant. As he rose slowly to his feet, pain flooded through his entire body. He was still thinking about what the young men had said.

It had been Councilor Shingu who had arranged for him to guard Taguchi, but why would Shingu want to reveal this to the men and have them attack him? It made no sense. To Jubei, it was a bewildering puzzle.

Stopping to rest many times, and finally crawling on all fours, he eventually reached the road. His eyes were accustomed to the dark, and he soon picked out the figure of a man lying there.

Feeling the body with his hands, he found that the man was dressed for traveling, with straw sandals and leggings, as well as a rope tied across his chest to hold the pack on his back. The body was undoubtedly that of Taguchi, and Jubei's fingers soon located a terrible gash from the shoulder to the chest. The cut had obviously been fatal, but just to make sure he felt for a pulse. As he had feared, he was too late. Taguchi was dead.

Groping further, he realized that the body had been searched and the man's pack had been opened.

So they got what they were after, he thought.

He sat down on the road, finding it difficult to think clearly. The pleasant young man he had met for the first time that day had lost his life as a result of his incompetence. Jubei hung his head in shame. Then he reached out and closed Taguchi's eyes before binding the wound in his own thigh.

Exhaustion and pain wracked his body. The lights in the town had by now dwindled in number, and he wondered miserably if he could manage to make it home.

When he finally reached his house, he hammered on the door, then slumped awkwardly into a sitting position. There was a glimmer of light inside, then Moto was standing before him.

"What happened?" she gasped, holding out a hand toward him. By the light of the candle she was carrying he looked a mess, caked in a mixture of mud, blood, and sweat.

"They got us. It was a trap."

"A trap?"

"We were ambushed."

As Jubei had been laboriously making his way home, half-walking and half-crawling, he had gone over the events repeatedly in his head. It had been a trap from the very beginning. That was the only logical conclusion he could find to explain why it had been "arranged" for him to be the escort.

"Anyway, we must get you inside."

"No," he replied, brushing aside her hand. He could not be sure if Councilor Shingu was part of the plot. If he was not, he would still be waiting up for Taguchi and Jubei. "I have to go to Shingu's residence and report to him."

"We must attend to your wounds first." Holding the candle in one hand, she bent down, wrapped her other arm around his waist, and lifted him up. She did this effortlessly, and he felt his feet leave the ground for an instant. Moto was large-boned but by no means a big woman—she was much smaller than Jubei, in fact, but her strength was prodigious. Jubei remembered the story of Moto carrying the millstones in one hand while holding her hair up with the other, and he thought ruefully that this must be how the stones had felt. However, it felt good to have her there to rely on. He thought of sending her to the councilor's home with a message, and at this the tension drained from his body, leaving him happy to cling to her shoulder as she half-carried him into the house.

"All the same, I am disappointed at the result. I believed you capable of better." Councilor Shingu looked scornfully at the sagging paunch of the man sitting before him—Jubei.

Moriya Ichinoshin was in the room with them and he apologized, saying it had been his fault for selecting the wrong man for the job. It was hard to tell whether he was shifting blame away from Jubei or covering up his own mistake, but Jubei was interested to learn that it had been Ichinoshin who suggested him as an escort.

"Well, it was obviously a poor choice," said Shiba Yahachiro, the chief censor, who was also present. "More than ten years have passed since Tsubuki Jubei was famous for his skill with the sword. Now he is old and not as agile as he used to be."

"It is hard to credit," the councilor said, not looking convinced. He could not reconcile Tsubuki's past prowess as a swordsman with his disastrous performance in the ambush. "A lot of skilled swordsmen his age boast of being able to hold their own against younger men. There's Wakamatsu Kihei, Tsugé Sanzaemon, Ogata Hikoroku . . ."

"Yes, but they lead sober lives and do not neglect to practice regularly," Shiba said, making Jubei feel uncomfortable. Shiba had a round, flat face and sported a mustache, despite the general dislike of facial hair. "Tsubuki Jubei limits his daily practice to the taverns of Hatsune—not much use in a fight." He seemed to think this highly amusing and let out a loud guffaw. Shingu gave a forced laugh, but Ichinoshin did not even smile. He looked tense, and his eyes remained fixed on Jubei.

"Anyway, judging from the size of his paunch, it must be some time since he last did any practice." Shiba added a final dig at Jubei before addressing him seriously. "I would like you to repeat to the councilor what you told me before." He gave Jubei permission to sit and stretch out his injured leg if it was too painful to remain kneeling.

While Jubei was still confined to bed with a high fever, Shiba had come to his house to question him about the ambush. Jubei had told the chief censor about the events of that evening, but Councilor Shingu had yet to hear the full story. Ichinoshin went to a corner of the room and returned with a small writing table bearing brushes, paper, and ink, so apparently he was there as a secretary to make a written record of everything that was said.

Although Jubei's wound was far from healed, he claimed his leg was better and continued to kneel despite the pain. Having already been made the butt of their laughter once, he did not want to make a greater fool of himself than necessary, so he bore the pain stoically.

"You say that the attackers emerged from the rice fields?" Shiba asked, moving his hands horizontally to convey a pincer movement.

"That is how it seemed to me, although it was too dark to see clearly."

"And the messenger, Taguchi"—Shiba dropped his gaze briefly before leaning toward Jubei—"did he have any premonition of the attack? Did he say anything?"

"I would not say he had a premonition, but he mentioned that when he left Edo he was warned of danger and told to be on his guard."

As he spoke, Jubei felt a cold rage building within him. He remembered how Taguchi had smiled with relief when he heard that Jubei had been sent by Councilor Shingu to be his escort. His anger was directed at his own ineffectiveness during the attack.

"How many men were there?"

"I cannot be sure, but I would say five or six."

"You say you injured one of them?"

"Yes."

"Where he was wounded?"

"In the left shoulder or upper arm."

Shiba looked over to check that Ichinoshin was writing all this down, then continued questioning Jubei about everything that had happened until he left the scene. Some of the questions merely repeated what he had asked Jubei when he visited him at home.

"Did you see their faces?"

"No, it was too dark."

"So you have no idea of their identities?"

"No."

Shiba sighed and looked down at the floor, fingering his mustache thoughtfully. "Can you think of anything else that might be helpful?" he asked encouragingly.

"Perhaps."

"What is it? If you can think of anything at all, we want to hear it."

"Well, I heard the men talking to each other."

"Yes, and what about it?"

"I think I recognized one of the voices." He could feel the eyes of both Ichinoshin, who had not raised his face until then, and the councilor fixed on him.

"Why did you not mention this the last time we spoke?" the chief censor demanded.

"It only occurred to me later."

"So whose voice was it that you recognized?"

"I cannot recall the name, but it's on the tip of my tongue."

"Do you think you will remember it later?"

"It will probably come to me when I least expect it."

"If it does, let me know right away," Shiba ordered.

He would no doubt be duly punished for his failure to carry out the task assigned to him, but neither the chief censor nor the councilor touched on that. Jubei was told that he could return to his post as soon as his wound had healed, and was given permission to leave. Outside, the sun was still shining, but people were already leaving their posts at the castle to go home. Twice he saw higher-ranking retainers, followed by their retinues, making their way toward their mansions at a leisurely pace.

Councilor Shingu's residence, enclosed within a wall, was in the area reserved for senior retainers and lay beside a wide road, now lit by the last rays of the setting sun. While Jubei had been confined to bed, the season had changed: the humid summer heat had cooled, and although intense the sunlight seemed weaker.

As Jubei walked away from the mansion, the tension in his body gradually receded.

I wonder if I managed to fool them, he thought. When he said that he had recognized the voice of one of the assailants, he had been setting a trap. He was convinced that the person who had planned the ambush—or someone connected to him—was a close associate of Councilor Shingu. It might be Shingu himself, who did not seem unduly upset by the loss of the letter, or Ichinoshin, who had selected him as escort, or even the chief censor, who had chosen to question him in private instead of going through official channels. There was nobody he could trust.

However, he was certain that whoever was behind the attack would not be able to ignore the trap he had set. Jubei would have to be silenced before he remembered the name of the man whose voice he had recognized. If his plan worked, something would happen that would reveal the person behind the plot.

He had no idea what he intended to do once he discovered the culprit or culprits, but he would surely make them pay. He wanted to avenge poor Taguchi Shozo, who had died through Jubei's inability to protect him. Jubei wanted to reclaim his reputation, and above all he wanted to make sure his income would not be further reduced.

Jubei walked up to the moat before taking the long way back to Shingu's mansion in Bandai. He slipped into an alley on the opposite side of the street, where he could get a clear view of the gate. In the time it had taken him to make the detour, the sun had already set and twilight was deepening in the streets.

At six o'clock Chief Censor Shiba emerged from the gate with a servant carrying a lantern, although it was still not that dark. Jubei made no attempt to follow him but continued watching from the shadows as he disappeared from sight.

The next person to leave was Moriya Ichinoshin. So much time passed before he appeared that Jubei feared he might have missed him while detouring around the moat. By then it was almost nine o'clock, yet although Ichinoshin carried no lantern Jubei was able to recognize him. A sliver of moon in the southwestern sky provided just enough light for Jubei to tail him. He remained close behind to make sure he did not lose him.

Ichinoshin walked straight to the moat, cut through another group of samurai residences to the bank of the Komochi River, and turned north without hesitation. Jubei, who had missed his evening meal, was becoming increasingly disheartened as he walked.

Of the three people he had met that day, Moriya Ichinoshin was his main suspect. Until today he had assumed that Ichinoshin had approached him at the tavern on Councilor Shingu's orders, but when he learned it was Ichinoshin who had suggested him in the first place, his suspicions were aroused.

It was not merely the fact that Ichinoshin had recommended Jubei, but that if it should be him everything seemed to make more sense. If Ichinoshin were working for somebody other than Shingu, he would want to report the latest developments to that person without delay, and Jubei was betting he would do it tonight.

That had been Jubei's motive when he started to follow him, but Ichinoshin seemed to be heading straight for his home in Sumiyoshi.

It looks like a waste of time, thought Jubei, his hunger gnawing at him more intensely. He guessed that Ichinoshin had eaten with Shingu, and the thought of the trust the councilor put in his subordinate made his suspicions appear groundless.

Just at that moment, Ichinoshin turned left away from the riverbank and headed back into town. He passed Mochizutsu, where members of the musket regiment and merchants had their homes, then cut through another samurai district in the direction of Aioi, close to the castle's northern gate. Like Bandai in the south, this was a district where many powerful retainers had their residences.

The waning moon was just bright enough for Jubei to see Ichinoshin hurrying through the deserted streets toward Aioi. It would have been much quicker to have followed the moat all the way, and the fact that he had chosen this circuitous route heightened Jubei's suspicions. With growing excitement Jubei wondered which house Ichinoshin would enter. The area beyond Aioi was where the daimyo's relatives lived.

Ichinoshin stopped outside a large gateway, and Jubei hastily ducked into the shadow of a wall. The young man looked back along the way he had come, then to the left and the right, before stooping and entering a low door to one side of the gate.

Jubei now realized who was behind the conspiracy. He knew who that house belonged to—Vice Councilor Usui Kuranosuke. It was almost disappointing how easily he had discovered the culprit.

Usui Kuranosuke had been born Sakamaki Yoshichiro, the eldest son of a lowly family with the hereditary title of lieutenant. The Sakamaki family had never produced anyone of prominence in the domain until Yoshichiro, whose intelligence caught the attention of the powerful Usui family. In the past, several Usui members had been appointed to the council of elders, and when they offered to adopt Yoshichiro into the family, he accepted at once, leaving his younger brother to succeed as head of the Sakamaki family. As he had hoped, he was soon given a seat on the council and was made vice councilor.

A huge disparity in rank now separated Jubei from Usui Kuranosuke, but when Usui was still known as Yoshichiro the two of them had studied the Mugai style of sword fighting together under Lieutenant Shiina Matazaemon. They were fellow students, but a few years later they became rivals for the hand of their teacher's daughter, Tatsu. Jubei had triumphed both in sword fighting and in love, for the wife he had lost a few years earlier had been none other than Tatsu.

As Jubei retraced his steps along the darkened streets, it dawned on him that this must be why Usui hated him. He could think of no other reason.

Usui had excelled at sword fighting, but Jubei always remained one step ahead. Usui had been awarded a certificate for his mastery of the Mugai sword fighting style, but it was Jubei who had been initiated into the school's secret techniques, an honor reserved for the best student. Usui had performed well in sword fighting contests with other schools, but it was always Jubei who attracted fame and attention.

Despite this, Jubei found it hard to accept that his marriage to Tatsu or his skill with the sword could be sufficient reason for Usui wanting him killed after all this time. Besides, they were miles apart in rank. Before being adopted by the Usui family, he had been head of the Sakamaki family, with an annual income of 1,750 bushels of rice, which though greater than Jubei's was still within reach. Now Usui was a vice councilor with an income of 5,000 bushels, while Jubei was merely a chief groom with 325 bushels, so the gulf between them was as wide as that between heaven and earth. For Usui to envy Jubei would be like a lion envying a rabbit.

Jubei reached the river and kicked a stone into the darkness, hearing it hit the water with a splash. He wondered whether Usui enjoyed toying with him because he had sunk so low, in much the same way that a cat plays with a mouse before killing it. If so, he had better be prepared for the consequences. At that moment an idea sprang into his mind and brought him to standstill.

No, it couldn't be! he thought.

Jubei had been dismissed from his position in the daimyo's guard and demoted to chief groom, with a decrease of 175 bushels in income after a letter from the daimyo to his family had disappeared while entrusted to Jubei's care. Both the letter and the box that held it had vanished in the short time it took him to make preparations to go out. At first it was thought to have been some sort of prank, but the letter was never found and thus the responsibility for losing it fell on him.

No sooner was he demoted for dereliction of duty than his luck took a turn for the worse: his wife died the following year.

This was at around the time that Usui had risen to prominence, and it now struck Jubei that maybe Usui had arranged for the letter to be lost.

I don't believe it! Jubei took a deep breath and started walking again. After all, he still did not know for certain if Usui had been behind the ambush. He would have to wait and see who took the bait he had prepared.

The following day Jubei reported back for duty, telling his superior that he had made a full recovery. His wound was almost completely healed, and though the leg was still a little stiff, it did not prevent him from working on his feet all day. Three days passed uneventfully, but on the fourth day Jubei worked a late shift and did not leave the castle until after nightfall.

One of the daimyo's favorite horses had come down with an infected hoof and was being treated by the horse specialist, who lanced the boil and disinfected it. Fortunately, the infection was not serious, but the hoof had to be kept cool twenty-four hours a day. The stableboys attended to the horse at night, but during the day the chief grooms worked shifts until ten o'clock at night, when the gate of the outer bailey closed.

That night it was Jubei's turn to stay late. He waited until he heard the temple bell of Kogakuji strike ten, then left the stables and walked across the dark outer bailey, passing the residences of the district steward and the daimyo's family. Apart from the light in the guardhouse, the outer bailey was pitch black, and not a soul was about. Jubei crossed the moat and entered the merchant quarter.

He walked through the quiet streets and crossed a bridge over the Komochi River. Just as he reached the other side he became aware that somebody was following him, not even bothering to hide the sound of their footsteps. He turned into a road along the riverbank and quickened his pace, only to hear the men behind him break into a run. There were three of them.

So they came after all, thought Jubei. He was amazed that they should be so open about it!

They obviously intended to silence him, which proved that Usui Kuranosuke was the one who had planned the ambush. It was Usui who had ordered Taguchi and Jubei killed and the daimyo's letter stolen, although Jubei could not imagine why he should have taken such a risk. For the first time he realized how deeply Usui hated him. Usui seemed to believe that he could have a lowly groom killed by simply crooking his little finger, but Jubei was determined not to let him have his way.

Coming to an alley, he dived into it and started to run. The footsteps behind him also picked up speed, so he turned another corner into an area filled with shops and merchants' houses that he knew well. Then he turned again, this time in the opposite direction.

The moon had doubtless risen by now, but luckily for Jubei it was hidden by clouds. At one point he came to a crossroads where a shadowy figure was lurking with a drawn sword. Jubei heard footsteps behind him and for a moment thought he was trapped, but he managed to escape and eventually eluded his pursuers completely. He reached home exhausted from these exertions.

However, Usui was not one to give up after a single foiled attempt. The following night, he ordered the assassins to Jubei's house.

It was Moto who first noticed the noise—a faint scratching sound, as if somebody were trying to prize open one of the shutters. She got up and dressed quickly. Taking a short sword from the wall cupboard, she slipped out of the room she shared with Fusae without waking the girl. If it was a burglar, she intended to put paid to him with a single blow.

She noticed one of the shutters moving slightly. The movement stopped and she heard someone take a deep breath. The next minute the shutter was silently lifted out of its groove and removed. With the shutter gone, a stream of pale moonlight flooded into the darkened house. Moto moved next to the opening, her sword raised and ready.

After what seemed an age, a head poked in. Before she had a chance to strike, however, it was withdrawn and replaced by a foot.

Moto gave a cry as she brought her short sword down, turning it at the last moment to hit the man's foot with the blunt side of the blade. Given her prodigious strength, she must have shattered the bones, for there was a strange sound as the foot was snatched away. This was followed by the noise of someone falling to the ground, but the person did not cry out. After that, silence returned, and Moto looked out to see two figures in black stumbling toward the gate. The man with the broken foot was being carried by his accomplice.

At this point Jubei came out of his room, woken by the noise.

"What happened?" he asked, looking out just in time to see the two figures disappear.

"It would seem that we were visited by burglars," Moto replied. She had already sheathed the short sword and asked Jubei if he was going to pursue them.

Jubei shook his head and said, "No, they weren't burglars."

"Then who were they?"

"Did you cut the man?"

"No, I used the back of the blade."

"Anyway, I had better put the shutter back."

As Jubei turned to go to the door, he asked Moto to light the lamp in the living room since there was something he wished to discuss. By the time he returned from checking that the house was secure, Moto was waiting there by the lamp.

"I believe that the two men you saw," he began, then paused briefly before continuing. "I believe they were assassins sent by Councilor Usui."

"What?"

The excitement of her encounter had brought a sparkle to Moto's eyes and a flush to her normally pale face. She had dressed in haste and the front of her kimono was slightly open, affording Jubei a glimpse of the whiteness of her skin. He looked at her with fresh eyes, never before having noticed how beautiful she was.

Perhaps reading his thoughts, she asked him sharply, "Why would Councilor Usui do that?"

Jubei hurriedly looked away from her bosom and began to explain. "It all began when I was given escort duty." He told her everything: his suspicions that Usui had specially selected him so he could be killed in the ambush, and the reasons why Usui loathed him. "So after he failed last night, he sent the assassins here."

Moto said nothing.

"He believes that his own life will be in danger if he doesn't silence me."

"So you think he'll try again?"

"Yes, we have to be prepared for that."

Moto sat looking down at her hands on her lap, then she lifted her eyes. "You cannot go against him alone. You have to tell Councilor Shingu everything."

"No." Jubei spoke without any hesitation. He had already given the matter a lot of thought. "It's true that this involves a plot against the domain, but as far as I'm concerned it's a private matter. The councilor is acting out of an old hatred for me. I'm not the man I was, I've lost my martial skills, and I've sunk to the post of chief groom. Despite that, he still wants to play with me as if I were a toy."

As he spoke, Jubei realized that this must have been exactly how Usui had felt when he laid his plans.

"He's repulsive!" Moto exclaimed, shocked by the depth of Usui's malice.

"I used to have a reputation as a swordsman, and I intend to finish this myself and not involve Councilor Shingu," Jubei said to explain his decision.

"But think of your age."

"First, I'll give up drinking. I won't be visiting Hatsune again for a long time."

"Good! You've been drinking too much recently."

"And I must get fit again. If I practice I should be able to handle Usui alone. But first I have to do something about this body," he said, gazing at his paunch reproachfully. He looked up, listening for the slightest noise, but Fusae and Kumé seemed to have slept through the night's events.

"I have only one concern," he continued. "I can look after myself, but I cannot keep an eye on the house when I'm on duty."

"You think we're in danger, too?"

"Yes. There is no telling how far Usui will go to have me silenced. I have to be prepared for the worst."

"Please don't worry," Moto replied quietly. "I may only be a woman, but I will look after Fusae and Kumé."

"Thank you. I'm relying on you."

He had never felt as close to Moto as he did at this moment. Had it not been for her, they might all be dead by now. She had become a vital part of the family.

In light of that, he thought, perhaps he should raise the subject of marriage. They would have to discuss it sometime, and now they were in tune with each other it was a good time. He cleared his throat.

"The other night you mentioned that you wished to discuss something with me. I thought we might do so now."

"No," she said, her expression at once cooling. "It is no longer necessary."

"There's no need to be like that."

"Talking about it now is pointless," Moto muttered, looking at the floor and frowning.

What is going on? Jubei wondered, bewildered by the change in her attitude. That's the problem with women, he concluded.

A lot had happened since she had asked to talk to him that evening, but obviously he should have heard her out then. No sooner had they felt an empathy for each other than he had to go and ruin everything. It was most disappointing.

"How long has it been since you were last here? Five years?" Shiina Matazaemon remarked sarcastically.

It hurt to be treated like this by his old sword fighting master and former father-in-law. Jubei hung his head.

"Actually it was at the end of last year. I came with Fusae."

"Oh yes, I'd forgotten. Your wife died, so you're no longer our son-in-law and it is not so important whether you come or not. But Fusae is our granddaughter, and I wish you'd bring her to visit us more often, if not for me, then for her grandmother."

"Forgive me. I will do so in the future."

Shiina Matazaemon had retired and his son, who was almost Jubei's age, had become head of the household and taken over his father's post as lieutenant. In rank, the Shiina family was higher than Jubei's, a fact reflected in the size of their garden. Large trees in it cast deep shadows, while the fluffy heads on the tall eulalia grass by the pond shimmered in the sunlight. Occasionally, a splash was heard as one of the prized carp leaped out of the water.

Beyond the pond, on the northern side, stood a huge old zelkova tree, and between it and the wall was an area of flattened earth, which was the practice ground where Matazaemon taught the Mugai style of sword fighting. He had mastered the technique while stationed in Edo, and on his return to the domain had received special permission from the daimyo to teach it in his spare time. Since he did not have a proper dojo, he never had more than five students, and more commonly just three.

Jubei and Usui had both studied sword fighting on that patch of land, one-third of which was visible beyond the zelkova. At the moment it was empty apart from the leaves that were falling from the tree.

"Why don't you get married again?" Matazaemon asked suddenly, causing Jubei to turn his gaze away from the garden. "Don't worry about us. It's not good for you to be single and doesn't help Fusae, either. You need to find a good wife."

"I agree."

"Now what was her name?" said Matazaemon, placing a finger on his pointed chin as he thought. "Don't you have Aiba's daughter living with you?"

"I do."

"How long is it since she moved in—ten years?"

"No, only five or six."

"Five or six years is long enough. From what I hear, Fusae thinks of her as a mother."

"So it seems."

"Then why don't you marry her?"

"Well, various reasons."

"Don't be ridiculous!" he barked. "That's no way for a forty-year-old man to talk. She's been living with you for years, so what's to stop the two of you getting married? You should either marry her or send her back to her parents. That's how a man should behave."

"You're quite right."

"If you go out drinking every night without putting your house in order, your reputation will suffer. You must pull yourself together, for Fusae's sake if not your own."

"Actually, I've not been drinking recently," Jubei said sheepishly.

"What do you mean?"

"I've given it up."

"What brought all this about?" said Matazaemon, looking at him dubiously.

"I've been thinking things over. I've given up drinking and I want to start sword fighting again. That's why I have come to you."

"Oh really," Matazaemon said scornfully. "I don't suppose that this has anything to do with that special job you accepted recently and failed in?"

Jubei looked at his father-in-law in shocked surprise. Councilor Shingu had gone to great lengths to keep the ambush a secret, and Taguchi Shozo's death had been recorded as due to illness. There was no way anybody could know of it.

"Where did you hear that?" Jubei demanded.

"I've got ears."

Jubei stared at him in silence.

"Well, I admit I don't know any details." Having spoken, the old man looked pointedly at Jubei's sagging belly. "But goodness knows what the person who offered you the job was thinking. And you're no better for accepting it. You don't bear the slightest resemblance to the Tsubuki Jubei I used to know."

Hearing this put so bluntly made Jubei's sheepish smile disappear. No sooner had he retreated moodily into silence than Matazaemon spoke again, remarking that Usui—he referred to him by his former name, Yoshichiro—was quite the opposite.

"He turned up here about a year ago to practice with me. He's almost as good as he used to be. I hear he works out with a wooden practice sword every morning—every single morning, mind you. When I asked him why, he just laughed and said he could not perform his duties unless he was physically fit. Practicing cannot be easy for a man in his position."

"I would agree with that," Jubei responded reluctantly, but his dislike of the man was such that his expression darkened at the mere mention of his name. Matazaemon failed to notice this and went on to add insult to injury.

"If you went up against him now, you wouldn't stand a chance. Hardly surprising, since only those who make the effort succeed. I bet you haven't practiced in years. You've done nothing but drink. And to think your sword fighting skills were once renowned throughout the domain, and you were expected to take over the dojo after me. What a waste!"

Jubei felt thoroughly humiliated. After being told he could not defeat Usui, he seemed deaf to whatever else was said. However, he managed to overcome his shame to plead with Matazaemon.

"I said I wanted to start again. Will you teach me?" He bowed deeply.

"It would be a waste of time," Matazaemon said coldly, looking Jubei over from head to toe. Finally he broke into a smile. "But if you're serious about it, I can hardly refuse. All right, I'll have Yasunosuke check you out."

Jubei agreed, although he could not hide his disappointment, for Yasunosuke was Matazaemon's youngest son. Matazaemon hurriedly explained that his back was troubling him and that Yasunosuke handled all the training now.

"Don't dismiss him too fast. Two times out of three he beats even me. He's better than his brothers."

Jubei went to the practice ground and removed his shoes. The feel of the sandy soil between his toes made him conscious that he had been neglecting something very important for too long. The cold earth felt good.

He looked over toward the zelkova. The rays of the setting sun hit the silvery trunk, creating a ruddy glow. His thoughts went back to the high-spirited girl who used to stand beneath it and watch him practice, the girl who grew up to become his wife. It all seemed so unreal now, as though it had happened in a different age. The years had passed and he had become overweight and ugly. He was filled with somber regret.

After the death of his wife, he'd been like a man possessed. Too young to be a widower, he found escape in the bars of Hatsune, searching for solace in a bottle. Over time he developed a liking for alcohol and started going there with the sole object of getting drunk. The memory of his wife's face had gradually faded.

Her death had been like a deep cut that had grown a scab but never truly healed inside, and occasionally it would leave him filled with sadness, just as he was now. He stood motionless on the practice ground as the leaves fell around him.

"Sorry to have kept you waiting," called a cheerful voice. Turning, Jubei saw Yasunosuke coming toward him with two wooden swords. He was tall and dashing with a ready smile, a good-looking young man of twenty-four or twenty-five who was waiting for some high-ranking family to adopt him and provide him with a post.

After exchanging greetings, Yasunosuke gave Jubei one of the wooden swords.

"Let's start with fifty strokes."

The sword felt quite heavy. Jubei raised it above his head with both hands and brought it down in an arc, stepping forward as he did so. He took a pace back and repeated the action. He did this again and again, and his breathing grew increasingly labored.

By the time he completed the fifty strokes, his clothes were soaked with sweat.

"How do you feel? Out of breath?" Yasunosuke asked, watching him closely and moving nearer as he was finishing.

"A little," Jubei replied. The truth was that he felt an overpowering thirst and was so short of breath he could hardly enunciate the words, but he could not bring himself to admit this.

When Yasunosuke saw that he had recovered sufficiently, he said brightly, "Let's do another fifty, shall we?"

"Another fifty?"

"Yes. Is that too many?"

"No."

Jubei swung the sword with all his might. His breathing soon became more labored than before, and he found himself gasping. His mind became blank and his legs trembled. As he brought the sword down for the final time, all thought of his reputation or appearances had been abandoned. Dropping the sword, he bent forward and put his hands on his knees. He was panting and wheezing, and the blood thundered in his ears.

This time Yasunosuke did not ask if he was out of breath.

"You need to get into shape before you think of brushing up your technique," he remarked bluntly. "But you might get somewhere yet."

Jubei looked up at Yasunosuke's encouraging remark.

"You think so?"

"Yes, I do. The way you swung the sword was impressive," Yasunosuke said to him with a friendly smile, implying that he could still glimpse the Jubei of old.

The theft of the daimyo's secret letter was never made public, and perhaps because Jubei could not identity his attackers, Usui's attempts on his life ceased.

From around November that year there were reports of a large, goblinlike figure glimpsed on cold moonlit nights racing up and down the riverbanks or leaping from one sandbank to another in the river itself. However, this was just Jubei taking Yasunosuke's advice and trying to get back in shape. That was about the only rumor of interest as the New Year dawned and snow began to fall. Throughout the long winter everyone went around with bowed heads beneath dismal gray skies as they waited patiently for spring.

By March, the winter's grip on the countryside was easing. The snow melted, the cold became more tolerable, and people began to look forward to the cherry blossoms. As the townsfolk became more active, two fresh rumors swept through the samurai district.

One concerned a heated argument—said to have occurred at the chief councilor's house—between Usui Kuranosuke and the chamberlain in Edo, Mitani Jinjuro, who had recently returned to the domain on a visit. Councilor Shingu apparently mediated between the two, but the cause of the dispute remained unknown.

At around the same time, the town magistrate, Sukegawa Jidayu, sent men to search the house of Shinkaiya, the merchant, and confiscated his books. Shinkaiya himself was subjected to two days of interrogation. This was alleged to be connected with the dispute at the chief councilor's house, although the object of the house search remained a mystery and no official announcement was made.

Immediately afterwards, however, both Usui and Shingu revealed that they were gathering supporters and creating rival factions within the clan. Jubei expected to be recruited by Councilor Shingu, but his previous failure had obviously been too much of a disappointment and no invitation came. Naturally, the Usui faction made no approach.

The other rumor concerned Jubei himself and how he had single-handedly stopped a runaway horse in the castle grounds. Word of this soon spread, but unlike the councilors' dispute, which was discussed in whispers with trepidation, the story about Jubei recapturing the horse was talked of openly. People felt there was something rather comical about the chief groom chasing a horse through the outer and inner baileys.

Of course, for Jubei the incident had been anything but a joke. The horse that had kicked a groom and escaped was a spirited black stallion named Taniarashi. Three stableboys had been grooming it in the exercise ground in the outer bailey when it bolted. Perhaps because Taniarashi was the only horse there that day, the gate had not been closed and the stallion galloped across the ground and away. The situation turned serious when the horse headed for the northern and most lightly guarded bridge in the castle, which linked the outer bailey to the inner bailey. Only one man was on duty there, and the gate on the other side was always left open during the day.

The shouts of the stableboys and the clatter of hooves on the flagstones brought the three chief grooms outside, and they immediately set off in pursuit of the horse accompanied by several stableboys. However, by the time the horse thundered over the bridge and into the inner bailey, Jubei was the only one who could keep up. The others had been left far behind. There were fewer buildings in the inner bailey, but a large crowd could usually be found in the vicinity of the main gate. Beyond that gate, one more bridge led to the inner castle keep.

If the horse were to enter the grounds of the keep, all the chief grooms would have no choice but to commit suicide in atonement. Jubei was running as fast as he could to catch up with the horse. Despite the great exertion necessary, however, he still had the presence of mind to note that the cherry trees along the moat would soon be bursting into blossom. The horse continued to gallop on under the cherry trees, covering half the perimeter of the inner bailey before coming into view of the people by the main gate. Seeing the demented horse dashing toward them, they scattered in all directions.

Jubei, forcing every ounce of strength from his legs, was gradually gaining on the horse. If anybody had seen him then, they would not have laughed. Rather, they would have looked on in awe and admiration. His face was bright red and his teeth were clenched as he drew level with the horse and caught its flowing tail. The horse neighed loudly and reared, swinging its body around to trample Jubei with its front legs. Man and beast faced each other.

Jubei was the faster. Reaching up, he seized the bridle with one hand and brought his other down on the horse's nose as hard as he could. The horse shook its head and tried to bite him, foam flying from its mouth. Jubei dodged nimbly this way and that, thwarting the horse while keeping his grip on the bridle. The horse eventually lowered its head and, after one last kick with its rear legs, grew quiet. At that point, the other grooms finally appeared and attached a rein to the bridle.

By the time Jubei had brought the runaway horse under control, he was almost at the main gate where a crowd had returned to watch. A murmur of admiration arose at the sight of the horse being led away, and some people clapped, probably merchants who had hurried outside to watch. It is doubtful if any of the people who applauded then or laughed on hearing the story later realized how fast Jubei had run. In order to overtake the horse, it meant that he had had to run faster than it.

But Jubei did notice. Not only had he been able to overtake a runaway horse but he was not even particularly winded. He was pleased that he had not embarrassed himself by collapsing from exhaustion.

It's all thanks to Yasunosuke, he thought. The day's events restored his badly bruised self-confidence, and when he returned home that evening he was full of pride in his physical prowess.

The only bedroom in the house had been given to Moto and Fusae, and Jubei slept in the living room. Being a widower for so long, he was used to sleeping alone, but that evening, when Moto helped him into his night clothes, as was customary, he caught her arm without saying a word. Moto looked up nervously. This had never happened before, and her first thought was that he had taken leave of his senses.

"Something has been troubling me," he said, his body still tingling with the exhilaration of the day's events. "You never told me what you wanted to talk about that night."

"It doesn't matter now."

"Yes, it does. Tell me."

"I had received an offer of marriage."

Jubei looked at her blankly. "Oh. I'm sorry I didn't talk to you then."

"It's of no concern."

Jubei was filled with remorse, and as this emotion grew he put his arm around her and pulled her toward him. Her body felt soft and warm.

"Don't ever leave me," he whispered. Seeing her nod, he added, "Come to me tonight when everyone's asleep."

Moto blushed, and with a gentle sigh she reached out and for the first time pulled him close. Perhaps because she had become used to him over the years, this time she made no remark about the smell of horses.

Jubei and one of the stableboys were rubbing down a horse when the drum sounded, signaling the end of the day's duties.

"Hey, Jubei!" his superior called out, emerging from his office next to the stables. "Is that going to take much longer?"

"No, we're nearly finished. Please don't wait for me."

The horse they were washing, using water from a barrel at one end of the stable block, was a three-year-old stallion that had just been ridden by the Master of Horses, Masé Gengo. He had praised the mount, saying it held great promise, but Jubei and the stableboy knew that already. The horse's black coat gleamed in the sunlight, and it arched its neck gracefully when cantering. When it galloped, it flew like the wind.

The horse had worked up a sweat and it narrowed its eyes in pleasure, shaking itself occasionally as it was being washed. Jubei was in no hurry to go home, and he was off duty the next day. Holding the wet brush in his hand, he stretched and looked around. The stables and their surroundings were already in the shade cast by the cedar trees beside the moat, but the sun still shone on the fence on the far side of the exercise ground. It was rare to see anybody walk in that part of the bailey, near the back gate, and today it was deserted as usual.

The sun hitting the branches of the pine trees in the inner bailey made the pine needles shimmer. Jubei looked up and noticed puffs of autumnal clouds drifting in the distant sky. When he turned his eyes back to the ground, the area around the stables seemed dark by comparison.

"Shall we call it a day, then?" he said to the stableboy. He raised his hand to undo the cord with which he had tied up his sleeves to keep them out of the way as he worked. As he did so, a strange heavy sound reverberated around the bailey, making him pause with his hand in midair. It resembled the roar of a typhoon or the cries of a great crowd, and seemed to be coming from the direction of the inner bailey. The noise showed no sign of abating.

"What's that?" Jubei asked, listening hard.

"Perhaps there's a fire," the stableboy replied, stopping his work and looking anxiously toward the old pine trees in the inner bailey. The sound came from that direction, out of their sight, where the main gate, the offices, and the residences of high officials were located.

Everybody had heard it. The other stableboys abandoned their games of chess, while foot soldiers and servants poured out to peer in the direction of the inner bailey. At that moment Jubei saw a group of people running with drawn swords from the barracks of the construction corps toward the main gate. The only buildings in the outer bailey that were visible from the stables were the construction corps barracks and a storeroom. Jubei realized immediately that something serious was afoot.

"You finish up," he said, rushing to retrieve his sword from the office before dashing barefoot toward the noise. Seeing this, his colleagues hurriedly followed him.

Running alongside the moat toward the main gate, he soon picked out individual voices, as curses, commands, names, and meaningless shouts became distinguishable from the background rumble. Suddenly he heard the clash of metal on metal and saw a crowd in the outer bailey by the main gate, moving first left, then right. He forced his way through the onlookers and caught sight of Vice Concilor Usui Kuranosuke in front of the pack.

Usui had removed his formal black outer garment and was clutching a bloodstained sword. His hair was in disarray and, with the sun on his face, he looked unnaturally pale. Two young samurai stood behind him, swords at the ready, guarding his back. They obviously belonged to his household or his faction. The three made their way slowly across the open space toward the outer gate. Surrounding them were ten young men, who all had their swords pointed at Usui. They appeared to be soldiers dispatched to arrest him. Feinting and probing, they were trying to find a weak point in his defense.

"Don't let them get out!" cried the officer in charge, obviously frustrated at the standoff. At this, the young men rushed into action.

Usui allowed the man in front of him to make his stroke, which he dodged easily by moving to one side. He parried a second blow with the back of his sword before delivering a well-timed swing that swept diagonally down toward the man's shoulder. Usui moved smoothly, and the stroke was executed with precision. His sword sliced deeply into his opponent, felling him. Death must have been instantaneous. Usui's party was not unscathed, though—one of the men behind him was down and the other wounded.

Usui continued to move forward steadily toward where Jubei was standing.

"What's going on?" Jubei asked an older, white-haired samurai next to him, never taking his eyes off Usui.

"Vice Councilor Usui was called to the castle to answer charges against him. When he was unable to talk his way out of the situation, he drew a sword and attacked his accusers. Councilor Tomita Manjiro died instantly, and Councilor Shingu was injured.

Jubei frowned.

"Why was he allowed to take his sword in with him?"

"I heard that someone in his faction called Moriya Ichinoshin threw Usui a sword from the corridor, although he was killed while doing so. A lot of blood has been spilled."

Jubei had his sword, still in its scabbard, in his hand. He slipped it through his sash, and pushed his way through the crowd, taking a position directly in front of Usui. Usui eventually recognized the man blocking his way and halted.

"Tsubuki Jubei!" He spat out each syllable, his hatred clear in his tone.

Hearing this, Usui's last retainer stepped forward to meet the challenger, but Usui stopped him. With a wave of his hand, he dismissed the soldiers attacking him. He was accustomed to being obeyed, and his peremptory gesture had such an air of authority that everyone instinctively fell back, although their swords remained pointed at him.

Jubei and Usui faced each other across thirty feet of empty ground. Jubei was barefoot and in his work clothes, his sleeves still tied back with the old cord and the wide bottoms of his baggy trousers tucked into his sash. Despite the fact that he had been exercising regularly, his paunch was still noticeable.

Usui looked like some demon from hell. His clothes were bloodsplattered, his hair was in disarray, and his face had a deathly pallor. His white footwear was filthy, too. As the two squared off, a hush fell over the crowd. People hardly dared to breathe.

"Jubei," Usui called, his lips curling into an evil sneer, "do you mean to stop me?" The sneer settled into a taut grimace as he renewed his grip on his sword. He took a step forward, then another, before raising his sword above his head and rushing toward Jubei, his face contorted with rage.

Jubei drew his own weapon and ran forward to meet him, their swords clashing as they passed each other. Stopping, they turned around and ran at each other again, their swords resounding with a metallic clang as they struck a second time. On their third pass, Jubei used a diagonal downward stroke, which was parried by Usui, who then tried to force Jubei's sword down. Knocking Usui's sword away, Jubei turned his sword so the blade faced up and held it low, a subtle change from defense to offense, a tactic that had been his specialty during his sword fighting days. He also altered his stance, which may have tricked Usui into believing that he had the upper hand over his old rival, for Usui stepped back and raised his sword to strike once more. The stroke was quick and powerful, and one he obviously thought would be decisive because a contemptuous smile once more formed on his lips. But he was wrong. As he struck downward, Jubei rushed in under the blow and made a deep cut into Usui's side as he moved past him.

Jubei turned to see Usui collapse to the ground. The sun still shone weakly through the branches of a zelkova tree in one corner of the area. The onlookers remained silent, transfixed by what they had witnessed.

It was past eleven o'clock before Jubei was able to return home that night. He arrived to find not only Moto at the front door to welcome him, but also Fusae and Kumé, who were usually asleep at that time.

"How did it end?" Moto asked. They had already heard some of what had happened at the castle. "We've been so worried."

"I was taken to the residence of the chief censor and questioned there for a long time. After that a messenger from Councilor Shingu arrived, saying I had to go and see him, too."

"Are you going to be punished?"

"It was not my place to tell them what I felt about Usui. The questioning was simply a formality. Councilor Shingu promised me a raise, so I hope to get back my original salary of 500 bushels of rice."

He assured them that there was no need for further concern and urged them to go to bed, but it took some time to convince them. Finally, he was able to enter the house. He was very tired and the wound on his arm was beginning to ache.

"Can you look at the cut on my arm?" he asked Moto as she followed him to his room to help him change. "And I'm starving. Is there anything to eat?"

Moto asked him to show her his arm, and relief flooded into her face when she saw the wound was only superficial. She threw her arms around him.

"I'm so glad you're safe," she said, burying her head in his chest and holding him tightly. He felt as though he were caught in a vise and his ribs were beginning to crack.

"Be careful or you'll have some broken bones to look after, too," Jubei whispered. He decided he had better marry Moto soon, or winter would be upon them once more.

Dancing Hands

When young Shinji came home from playing with his friends, he found a large crowd gathered in the narrow street where he lived. Most were women from neighboring houses, and Shinji soon spotted his mother among them. But there were also three men wearing long jackets whom Shinji had never seen before.

The women and the men in jackets were all looking in the same direction. Occasionally, one of the women would turn and whisper a few words to the person next to her before resuming her vigil. The object of their attention was the front door of Isaburo's house, which was wide open.

Not all the spectators were adults. Shinji noticed some children, even younger than himself, who were holding their mothers' hands and also staring at Isaburo's house. However, as nothing seemed to be happening, they eventually began scampering around the adults, weaving in and out among them like a pack of mice until cautioned by their mothers with a sharp tap on the head.

Shinji made his way over to his mother.

"Why is everybody looking at Okimi's house?"

"They did a moonlight flit," she replied, not taking her eyes off the door.

"What does that mean?"

"The family ran away during the night."

Shinji felt his heart lurch. Okimi was eight years old, two years younger than himself, and she was Isaburo's only daughter. They were good friends and had played together since they were little. He was just about to ask if Okimi had run away too, when a man emerged from the house. It was someone Shinji knew well—Seiroku, the landlord. He was plump and red-faced, and the little hair he had left on his head was pulled up into a tiny topknot. He walked over to the men in jackets and, without saying a word, shook his head.

"No change?" asked the tallest of them, a thin, elderly man.

Seiroku shook his head again.

"I asked again and again, but she won't answer. She just lies there with her eyes shut."

"You sure she's not asleep?" one of the other men ventured, but Seiroku shook his head firmly.

"No, she can hear me alright. When I asked her where Isaburo had taken his wife and daughter, she started to cry."

"The poor thing," said one of the housewives. She was plumper than Shinji's mother, and her voice had a surprisingly childlike quality. The women had been listening to what the men were saying, but suddenly they broke into a general chatter.

"What kind of people would do a thing like that? Disappearing in the night and leaving an old woman behind."

"Who would think it of Okatsu?"

"She seemed so good-natured. Who'd have guessed she would turn out rotten?"

"She had us fooled all along."

"Not so fast! You're being too hasty. They must have had a good reason to run off and leave the old woman behind."

"Of course they had a good reason. Isaburo may have looked like he was good at business—being smart and a smooth talker—but he had a gambling habit."

"I'd never have guessed."

"Well, he did. And no matter how hard Okatsu worked she could never keep up with his debts."

"That's got nothing to do with it," a deep voice boomed in reply. It was the tinker's wife, whose sunburned face was as dark as her husband's. "I could never leave an old woman alone like that, no matter what."

"That's true." Two or three voices chorused agreement, and with that encouragement the sunburned woman looked at the circle of women around her.

"It would be bad enough leaving the old lady if she were physically fit, but she can barely manage to get to the toilet down the street. And she spends the whole day in bed. Isn't that so, Omatsu?"

"Yes, she sleeps all the time," a slow-speaking woman replied. Omatsu lived next door to Isaburo and was a day laborer like her husband, Sukezo, but she was not working that day.

"If they're going to leave a bedridden old woman to fend for herself, they might just as well have killed her and have done with it," said the tinker's wife indignantly. The other women nodded, agreeing that nobody could be blamed for assuming that the family meant her to die. One woman asked about the family's pots and pans and bedding, and what had become of them. The high-pitched voice could only belong to the plasterer's wife, Okura.

"They must have left their pots and pans behind," another responded. "They can't have taken everything with them." She went to check with the landlord.

"They took everything," Seiroku replied. "Pots, pans, bedding—even the family altar. The only thing they left was the old woman."

The way he said this made the women burst out laughing. Some of them tried to imagine what it would be like if it were their own mother-in-law who had been left lying alone in a bare room. It was pitiful, certainly, but it had a funny side, too.

Shinji tugged at his mother's sleeve.

"Why is everyone laughing?"

"Because Granny is still there," his mother replied, her eyes twinkling with amusement as she looked down at him. "You know who I mean—the old lady with a face as wrinkled as a prune."

"Yes, I know her. I talk to her sometimes."

At this point the landlord came over, saying he had something he wished to discuss with them all.

"It's about Isaburo's old mother. We can't just leave her there like that."

Shinji pulled his mother's sleeve again.

"What is it?" she asked.

"I'm hungry."

"If you're out playing all day and don't come home for dinner, what do you expect? There's nothing left," she said, giving his head a poke with her finger, but when he started to snivel her expression softened. She told him there was some rice gruel in the pot in the kitchen and he could go and help himself.

Back at his house, he emptied the gruel into a bowl, took the pickle jar down from the shelf, and carried the bowl and jar into the front room. The paper-covered window of the kitchen was open halfway, letting the evening sun shine in. Shinji ate his dinner sitting in a pool of light.

It was still only February, but there was no wind, so even with the kitchen window open it was not cold. Shinji was hungry and quickly wolfed down the gruel.

Once he had finished, his thoughts returned to the disappearance of Isaburo and his family. Okimi's face rose in his mind. Among the children living in the alley, there were some he got on well with and some he did not. Okimi had been a good friend of his, and when they were small they had often played in each other's houses from morning till night. Looking back, he realized that he had not seen much of her lately.

It was not that they had fallen out. When Shinji turned ten and Okimi was eight, they had naturally become aware that he was a boy and she was a girl and that they were different, without really understanding why. And once this happened, it was no longer possible for them to spend all their time playing together as they used to.

Moreover, Shinji's world had recently expanded since he had

made friends with the boys living on the main street, and at some point he had stopped playing with Okimi altogether. Hearing that Isaburo and his family were gone forever, though, he felt he had made a terrible mistake in not spending more time with her. He wondered if it were true that she would never come back. As he did so, it was as if a dark shadow had suddenly fallen across him, blocking out the early spring sunshine. He remembered the dry fragrance of Okimi's hair and felt her dark, strangely grownup eyes watching him from somewhere.

Shinji was woken late that night by a loud shout. He looked around the room. The lamp was still lit, but there was no sign of his mother or father. Another sharp cry rang out.

Getting out of bed and sliding open the door of the room, he saw that the front door was ajar and the alley was flooded with light. He quickly dressed, slipped into his sandals, and rushed outside.

As he had guessed, the street was filled with people, and he could see their faces clearly by the light of the lanterns they carried. He ran toward the brightest cluster of lights to find a crowd gathered once again around the door of Isaburo's house.

Another shout was heard. It came from inside the house. Hearing it, the crowd began to mutter angrily.

"What kind of men would bully an old woman?"

"They're not human. Look at all the men standing around here! Can't they do something about it?"

Egged on by the shrill tones of the women, a lone man entered Isaburo's house. He was big, and even from behind Shinji could tell it was his father. His mother called out to him to be careful.

"Hey, you two in the house," he shouted. Shinji was impressed by the strength of his father's voice. "Leave the old woman alone. Surely even a couple of idiots like you can see you're not going to get a penny out of her."

A stream of curses issued from within the house. It was a deep, evil voice, the sort to make one's blood run cold. The man responsible was apparently moving toward the front door, for his voice grew louder.

"Are you the guy with the big mouth?"

"What if I am?" Shinji's father replied. Shinji felt his heart race with excitement. He could hardly breathe.

"I'll show you what!" There was the sound of wood creaking under strain, then the door burst open and two figures fell into the street. A shout rose from the crowd, and another young man rushed out of the house. Seeing the two men tussling on the ground, he made as though to draw a dagger, but before he could do so Sukezo, the laborer, caught his arm while Chogakubo, the priest, jumped on him. The tinker's wife started to rain blows on him that would put any man to shame. Sukezo was small and thin, but his muscles had been tempered by years of hard work. Pinioning the man's arms behind his back, he held him fast while the blows continued.

Meanwhile, Shinji's father was still wrestling with the other man on the ground. The gangster may have been no coward, but neither was he a match for a carpenter used to carrying heavy lumber.

Eventually, the gangster managed to break free and get to his feet, but his legs were trembling so much that running was out of the question. The crowd moved in on him, cursing and punching, until he collapsed to his knees as someone kicked him from behind.

"That's enough!" Shinji's father said, straightening his muddied clothes. The crowd slowly drew back from the men, and three housewives hurried into the house.

"What do you think you're doing, bullying an old woman like that?" Shinji's father demanded.

The man on his knees looked furtively at the people encircling him, his eyes as cold as a snake's, before turning to Shinji's father again.

"Isaburo has debts. We were sent to collect them."

"How much does he owe?"

"Ten gold pieces."

"And you thought you could get it from a bedridden old woman?"

"Isaburo's not here. We had no choice."

"Don't talk like a fool!" Shinji's father burst out angrily. "Go and tell your boss that Isaburo has done a flit and there's no one left except a decrepit old woman. If he's any kind of man, he's not going to tell you to take it out on her."

"We'll be in for it if we go back with nothing."

"Don't be stupid! Do as I say and we'll let you go. If not, we'll hand you over to the constables. Which is it going to be?"

Shinji was just about to go out to play when his mother called him back.

"Come and sit down."

He went and knelt in front of his mother, who stared at him in silence. Something must be troubling her because she looked worried.

"What's wrong?"

"You know Okimi's Granny, don't you?"

"Yes."

"I thought so. She often looked after you when you were little."

Shinji remained silent, wondering what all this was about.

"Whenever I needed to go out, I would leave you at her place. She used to give you rice crackers and tell you stories, remember?"

Shinji nodded. He remembered it very well. When he was left at Okimi's house, her grandmother would always make them something good for lunch.

"Well, if you heard that the Granny who used to look after you has stopped eating, you'd be worried, wouldn't you?"

Shinji said nothing.

"She's not eaten a thing since yesterday, no matter what I take her. She even refuses to drink water."

"Why won't she eat?"

"I don't know. That's the problem."

The landlord had said that even if Isaburo was a good-for-nothing, he could not believe that his wife would abandon the old woman like that. They may have run away, but he was sure they would come back for the old lady sooner or later, so he decided to let her remain in the house and had asked the people living nearby to look after her.

After talking things over, Shinji's mother and the tinker's wife were chosen to care for the old woman since they were at home during the day. It was not as if she were sick, so they would not have to do much more than bring meals to her three times a day.

However, it was not that simple. To their great surprise, the old lady stayed in her bed and would not even look at them when they entered the room. When they tried coaxing her to eat, she ignored them. They thought she might be embarrassed to eat in their presence, so they left the food there, but when they returned they found the tray untouched.

That proved too much for the short-tempered tinker's wife.

"Who does she think she is? Here we are, looking after her out of the kindness of our hearts and she doesn't even make an effort to eat. Well, I've had enough. If you want to take the trouble, she's all yours. If not, you'd better let the landlord know. Do whatever you like."

However, Shinji's mother could not bring herself to give up. She was worried that having been abandoned by her family, the old woman might have decided to die. A day and a half had passed since Isaburo's disappearance and she had not eaten a single grain of rice or drunk any water in all that time. There was no telling what she was thinking, but if Shinji's mother were to give up on her now, she would definitely die. Instead of losing her temper like the tinker's wife, Shinji's mother tried to think of a way to persuade the old woman to eat.

She knew she would not be able to accomplish much by herself and called on her neighbors to help, but to no avail. The old woman kept her mouth shut as tight as a clam and would not even open her eyes to look at the women.

"If we don't do something soon, she'll die for sure."

Shinji stared wide-eyed at his mother.

"That's why I thought you could take her the food."

"Me? Why me?"

"She always liked you, so if you took her the food and asked her to eat, she might have a little. It may not work, but I think it's worth a try."

Shinji picked up the tray, which was covered with a piece of cloth, and left the house. There was a bowl of rice gruel his mother had heated up, salted plums, pickles, and some hot soup. It was a simple meal, but to Shinji it looked tempting. He was halfway down the alley when a younger boy came out of a neighboring house and saw him carrying the tray.

"What's that, Shinji?"

"It's lunch for Okimi's Granny. It's my job to take it to her."

As he said this, he became aware of the importance of the role that had been entrusted to him. His mother had said that Okimi's grandmother was refusing to eat, no matter how much people pleaded with her, and it had fallen to him to try and persuade her. In other words, the grownups had all given up and everything now depended on him. He was glad to do what he could. Despite his youth, he was also concerned about Okimi's grandmother, and for the past two days he had been unable to pass her house without glancing inside.

He was sure she would eat if he were to ask her. As his mother had said, he was far from being a stranger to her, and, with her family gone, he was probably closer to her than anybody else.

Everyone will be so surprised when they hear that it was me who got Granny to eat, he thought to himself. She has to eat, otherwise she'll die, just like Ma said.

Nevertheless, he was slightly nervous as he entered Okimi's house. Coming in from the bright sunshine, the darkness inside made him feel as if a blindfold had been placed over his eyes. However, he was soon able to make out the stained paper of the sliding door, which was half-open, and the corner of a bedding quilt beyond it. Taking care not to trip, he went into the room and sat by the futon. He looked around. When he used to come over to play, the room had been so full of things that there was hardly any space to walk, but now it was completely empty apart from the bedding on the floor. He remembered his father remarking that Okimi's family could not have taken everything in a single night and must have started moving out their possessions much earlier.

No sunlight reached this inner room, with its worn tatami mats and the old woman lying in one corner. Even to Shinji it seemed cold and uninviting.

"I've brought you some food, Granny," he said. Only her face could be seen poking out from beneath the bedding. She was lying face up, but her eyes were tightly shut and she neither spoke nor looked at Shinji. Her hair was completely white and her face seemed tiny, the sunken cheeks crisscrossed by a mesh of wrinkles. Shinji noticed her cheeks moving slightly as she breathed, but apart from that there was no sign that she was alive.

"Please sit up and have some food," he began again. He pushed the tray toward her and moved a little closer. "I've brought you some rice gruel and pickled plums. The gruel's still hot." But she did not open her eyes, and only her hollow cheeks moved a little.

Shinji did not know what to do next. If he took the tray home and told his mother she would not eat, that would be the end of the matter; but he also knew that he could not leave the old woman in such a state.

It was the sight of her disarrayed hair that made him feel that way—that and her small pale face and wizened cheeks. Although everyone called her Granny, he had heard that she was not Isaburo's mother but his mother's mother, in other words, Isaburo's grandmother. That meant she was Okimi's great-grandmother. Shinji had no idea how old she was. All he knew was that she was ancient. There were other grandmothers living in the same alley, but none was as old as Okimi's, who had shrunk back to child-size and could hardly walk.

As Shinji looked at her lying there, neither speaking nor eating, a wave of sadness swept over him. He felt he understood vaguely how she must feel. He wanted to comfort her but could find no words to do so. He wanted to tell her that she would die if she did not eat, but he did not know how. His eyes filled with tears and he began to sob.

"What's wrong, Shinji?" came a weak but clear voice. Shinji looked up and saw her looking at him. He hurriedly wiped away his tears, but he was so overjoyed that she had spoken that his sobs gave way to loud wails as he heard her voice.

"Are you upset because I won't eat the food you brought? There, there, don't cry. Come around behind me and help me sit up."

Shinji ran out of the alley and into the main street, only to come to a sudden halt. The two men who had been bullying Isaburo's grandmother a couple of days ago were there, leaning against the wall of a store selling condiments. Their eyes were fixed on the entrance to the alley. They must have seen him come out, but neither of them said a word. Shinji lowered his eyes as he passed, but they did not try to stop him.

"This is getting ridiculous. Why don't we call it a day and go to Shin-Ishiba for some fun," the younger man said.

"Just keep your mouth shut and your eyes open, idiot," the other replied.

Shinji heard the men talking behind him, and though he did not understand much of what they were saying, he realized they were watching the house in case Okimi's parents returned. He broke into a run.

A friend from another part of town had come to his house to play that day and had left a book behind, so Shinji was hurrying to return it to him. It was already quite late, and he knew it would be dark by the time he got home. This and the fact that he wanted to get away from the men as quickly as possible spurred him to run faster. On the way he almost bumped into a man who shouted at him to look where he was going, but he did not slow down.

Shinji's friend, Matsutaro, was the son of a seed merchant and he had left his book of fairy tales at Shinji's house. Matsutaro had a lot of interesting books and occasionally even brought some grownup ones with pictures that Shinji had to keep hidden from his parents, so he was a friend worth keeping. If he returned the book straightaway, Matsutaro might bring him more in the future.

"Shinji!" Somebody suddenly called out his name and he stopped in his tracks. He had just entered the district adjoining his own. Everything was already bathed in the deep orange glow of the setting sun.

It was a woman who had called his name, but with the sun behind her it was difficult to see her face. Still, Shinji recognized her voice and silhouette immediately. It was Okimi's mother.

"Where're you off to?"

"I'm going to Matsutaro's house. Where are you going?"

Okimi's mother heaved a deep sigh.

"I thought I'd go and see how Granny's doing."

"You mustn't do that," Shinji said quickly, catching her by the sleeve and pulling her to the side of the street. "They're watching your house," he whispered.

"Watching our house?" Her eyes widened in surprise. "I should have guessed," she said.

"Don't go today."

"No, I'd better not."

Her gaze dropped to the ground and she looked pensive for a moment.

"How is Granny?" she asked.

"She's fine. She's eating."

"I feel bad about giving everybody so much trouble," she said to the ten-year-old, then sighed deeply again. "We meant to take her with us, but there wasn't enough time. Was the landlord very angry?"

Shinji watched her in silence.

"Shinji, can you keep a secret and not tell anyone you saw me here?"

"Okay."

"Thanks. And tell Granny that we'll come to fetch her as soon as we can, but make sure nobody hears you."

"Okay."

Okimi's mother gave him a small parcel, telling him it was Granny's favorite rice cake. Then, with a gesture of thanks, she turned and walked away, her plump figure soon disappearing into the dusk. Shinji had not even had a chance to ask about Okimi.

After he told Granny about meeting Okimi's mother and passed on her message, the old woman regained her appetite. However, days passed and still there was no sign of Isaburo or his wife.

A month later, just after the cherry blossoms had fallen from the trees, Shinji was coming home after playing with his friends. It was dark by the time he reached the gateway to the alley, and the thought of the scolding he could expect for having stayed out so late made him slow down and hang his head. But he soon quickened his pace again as he walked up the alley. A few houses already had their lanterns lit, while others were still dark. The clouds overhead, tinted by the last rays of the sun, gave enough light for him to see his way. The winter chill had dispersed and the air was pleasantly warm. There was not a soul about.

As Shinji passed Isaburo's house, he suddenly came to a halt, unable to believe his eyes. The front door of the house was sliding open slowly and silently, making the hairs on the nape of his neck stand on end. He knew that it could not be the grandmother because she was always in bed by the time the sun set. The door opened wider and a man stepped out. He had a grin on his face.

"Hey, Shinji!"

It was Isaburo. He was a tall, handsome man, and even in the twilight he looked rather dashing. He was carrying someone on his back—his grandmother.

"I heard what you did, Shinji. Thank you so much. Give my regards to your parents."

Saying that, he hitched the old lady higher on his back.

"Here we go then," he said to her, and he began to lope down the street with an almost clownish gait. His grandmother, bound tightly to his back, raised both her arms and waved them over her head, twirling her hands in time with his steps, just as if she were performing a dance that she remembered from her youth. Shinji saw how happy she looked on Isaburo's back and suddenly felt like laughing out loud. He no longer worried about the scolding he was in for. Raising his own hands above his head, he waved them back and forth as he capered homeward with the same merry step.

(英文版) 藤沢周平短編集
The Bamboo Sword and Other Samurai Tales

2005年11月21日　第1刷発行

著　者　　藤沢周平
訳　者　　ギャビン・フルー
発行者　　富田 充
発行所　　講談社インターナショナル株式会社
　　　　　〒112-8652 東京都文京区音羽1-17-14
　　　　　電話　03-3944-6493（編集部）
　　　　　　　　03-3944-6492（マーケティング部・業務部）
　　　　　ホームページ　www.kodansha-intl.com

印刷・製本所　　大日本印刷株式会社

落丁本・乱丁本は購入書店名を明記のうえ、講談社インターナショナル業務部宛にお送りください。送料小社負担にてお取替えします。なお、この本についてのお問い合わせは、編集部宛にお願いいたします。本書の無断複写（コピー）、転載は著作権法の例外を除き、禁じられています。

定価はカバーに表示してあります。

© 小菅和子 1981 1980, 1976, 1979, 1976, 1980, 1987, 1988
English translation © Gavin Frew 2005
Printed in Japan
ISBN 4-7700-3005-3

OHIO UNIVERSITY LIBRARY

Please return this book as soon as you have finished with it. In order to avoid a fine it must be returned by the latest date stamped below. All books are subject to recall after two weeks or immediately if needed for reserve.

CF